Too Big For His Roots

by John F Mc Loughlin

By the same author:

Is it four o 'clock yet?

You, me and Destiny

Chapter 1

Looking uncomfortable in his grey, chalk-stripe suit, Robert O'
Connor stepped off the train, his head held high and his face firmly
set in a show of defiance. He would never win any popularity
contests in Dromahair, but that did not bother him. The person
Robert most wanted to see on the platform was Katie, his faithful
girlfriend who had waited two and a half years for his return.
Hopefully, his parents had forgiven him for his decision to take the
King's Shilling and would also be there to welcome him home.

For days Katie Higgins rehearsed her words of welcome. However,
at the first glimpse of her returning soldier, those words deserted her
as she excitedly ran to greet him. Robert dropped his kit bag and
threw open his arms to embrace her. Grabbing her, he pulled her
close in a wonderfully firm embrace. When he finally loosened his
grip, Katie took a step backwards and luxuriated in a long, lingering
look at the man she had not seen for such a long time.

She had never seen her boyfriend in a suit and was not quite sure
what to make of the look. Robert seemed to read her mind. He felt
very self-conscious in the ill-fitting attire the army had provided for
his return to civilian life.

'I know I look a proper eejit in this oversized get-up'.

Katie laughed at the sight of her country boy in such an outfit.

'You look like a bank manager who lost weight in a hurry'.

'These demob suits are something else. There are only two sizes, too big and too small. Anyway, I'm sure you will be keen to pull these trousers off me later'.

Katie slapped him playfully on the arm.

'In your dreams, Robert O'Connor!'

'You wouldn't deny me that, Katie. My tongue is hanging out for a bit of action'.

Katie had long since determined that she would have a wedding ring on her finger before any man would get up close and personal with her.

'I thought the war would have given you more than enough action'.

Robert held her at arm's length as his eyes became reacquainted with the alluring contours of her delightfully chiselled body.

'Your enticing body is like a massive feast to a hungry man', he declared.

'Are you saying that I am massive?'

'You know well what I meant'.

Despite her feigned displeasure, Katie took this remark as the compliment he had intended.

It was reassuring to know that he still fancied her.

She recalled how they first met during an EXCUSE ME dance in the village hall in Dromahair. Robert had cut in mid-dance to claim her. Back then, he was bold and confident and so attractive.

Earlier that night, she had caught his eye as he powerfully steered a young girl on an exuberant circuit of the dance floor. Katie planned to invite him to dance whenever they announced LADIES' CHOICE, but she feared she might be swamped in a rush. It was fortunate that he had spared her from making her declaration of interest. The man was vain enough already.

Robert seemed to like her too, and they danced together for the rest of the night.

They started to date and continued to do so until he enlisted in the army.

Now that he had returned, Katie was relieved to see that her man looked fit and healthy. There was not even a scratch to blemish his strong, manly features. Whatever damage the war might have done to his mind, she was grateful that his body had escaped unscathed. Katie felt that the military drilling had improved his posture and accentuated his 5 ft. 11in frame.

Although his looks had matured, he was still the handsome and beguiling young man who had confidently burst into her life four years previously.

Just then, she felt that same tingle of excitement as he came back into her life.

Robert seemed equally enthused.

'Katie, I had to pinch myself to check that we are really back together'.

She wondered whether Robert had noticed any change in her.

'I suppose, like a visiting auntie, you'll tell me I got big since you saw me last'.

Whatever changes he may have observed, Robert was far from disappointed.

'You're even more woman than I recall', he announced as he pulled her close again and kissed her lustfully on the lips.

'Stop it, I say. Are you forgetting where you are?'

'I know only too well where I am, but I have to say I'm very disappointed that there isn't a brass band here to welcome me. Tell me where is all my family? Don't say that they have completely disowned me'.

No other O'Connor was on the platform, but that did not reflect the true situation. His brother, Edward, had agreed to collect him, but Katie had asked him to delay his arrival at the station to give her more time with Robert.

'Edward is outside with the donkey and cart. I asked him to delay his arrival a bit. He said he had to nip to the Co-operative Store for a few things anyway'.

That store was adjacent to the creamery where Robert had worked for fifteen shillings a week in pre-war times. His job had been to unload creamery churns from the local suppliers and record the quantity and quality of their milk. Robert was efficient at his job but was known to antagonise some farmers.

'That would be our Edward sitting out on a donkey cart while life passes him by. Is he as boring as ever, or has he livened up while I have been away?'

Katie would hear no criticism of Edward. He had been a great support to her during Robert's absence.

'He's still the same kind man. Alice and he are still going strong, and there could be plans for a wedding before long'.

'Well, I pity Alice wasting her life on that dozy bastard'.

Now that Robert had safely returned from the war, Katie was determined that there would be no more talk of travelling abroad again. Katie had plans for Robert, and it was now possible for her to dream about a happy life together.

'I kept all of your letters', she disclosed, with tears of joy beginning to well up in her light blue eyes.

'And I read them all about one hundred times', she added.

Robert seemed surprised at that revelation. He had forgotten most of what he had written in those letters.

'I could have written anything. A man thinks strange thoughts when death is all around him'.

Those letters were precious to Katie. Had her family home caught fire, at any stage, over the last couple of years, those letters were the only possession she would have risked her life to save.

The government censors had frequently redacted entire paragraphs of those letters, but such censorship had never bothered Katie. She was only interested in the personal details.

Without warning, the emotion of the moment prompted an outburst of unexpected gratitude on Robert's part.

'Thanks for waiting', he uttered with total sincerity.

'I am a lucky man, Katie and I know it', he said, reaching for her hand.

A young man close to the exit had observed the touching reunion.

'Be careful, Katie. Think of where his hands might have been'.

The remark provoked Robert to retaliate.

'Go home, Murphy, you little runt. A little lad like you should never be let out on his own'.

The young lad knew that his jibe had the desired effect.

'You are very funny, Corporal O'Connor, but I have the last laugh. You might not have heard, but I landed your old job in the creamery'.

Robert presumed that someone had filled the position but was never told who it was.

'And, what's more, you're not getting it back, you miserable turncoat'.

There had been a chequered history between Robert and the lad's older brother.

Robert had been targeted and could not resist returning fire.

'Mind you don't fall into one of the ten-gallon churns. A midget like you could be lost for days before anyone would notice'.

'Laugh away, but while you were off doing the King's dirty work, I was making good money there. The manager says I'm far more reliable than you and a hell of a lot less awkward', he added.

Money was something that Robert could do with too. He had earned up to a hundred pounds a year in the army but had blown most of it playing cards or drinking to excess when on leave. His excuse had been that the next bullet might kill him, so he should enjoy life while he had it.

Although Robert had been half-expecting a hostile reception from some, he was surprised that it had started before leaving the station building.

The incident served as a reminder to him that he had just joined the ranks of the unemployed in Eire.

That was a sobering thought.

Chapter 2

After a few moments, Edward O' Connor arrived on the platform.

'Well, if it's not my big brother, how are you?' he asked, extending his hand in greeting. The O' Connor brothers had never been close and had seldom seen eye to eye on anything. Edward was the serious and dependable young man with Robert being the flippant and volatile one.

'So, you're back then', Edward muttered.

'Ah, there's no fooling you', Robert cheekily replied.

'And I had a very pleasant trip too. Thanks for asking', he sarcastically added. Robert could not hide his disappointment that his father had not seen it fit to come to the station.

'So, the old man wasn't tempted to come to collect me?'

Edward scoffed at the suggestion.

'No, he wasn't. You are lucky that I'm here at all and luckier still to have Katie Higgins waiting for you', he added, looking to the girl for support.

Katie was so thrilled to have Robert by her side that she had not been listening to the exchange.

'Don't you worry about Katie and me. You should concentrate on your relationship with Alice Kelly. If you had any sense, Alice would be Mrs O' Connor by now'.

Edward did not welcome such advice from his brother.

'Alice and I are doing just fine, thank you', he snapped.

Robert might only have stepped off the train a few moments earlier, but normal service with his brother had been resumed.

'I am awful glad to hear that, Big Brother. That was one thing on my mind when the shells would be raining down around me'.

Edward would have been better to ignore such sarcasm, but he had never been able to do so. Robert O' Connor could wind his older brother up faster than he could wind his pocket watch.

'Do you realise this girl could have been matched up half-a-dozen times since you left, but for some daft reason, she preferred to wait for you?'

'Wise, bloody woman!' Robert replied.

Despite knowing Katie to be a very attractive woman, Robert, in his complacency, had never seriously considered rival suitors. Now, he recognised that other lads must have tried to exploit his absence. He was determined to identify those opportunistic predators. A few slaps would sort out even the best of them.

Robert wondered if Katie had been seriously tempted to stray. In the last year he had thought about her a great deal, as he had been close to death on several occasions. He had probably taken her for granted, but was determined this would never happen again. In his more reflective moments, Robert fully appreciated how much Katie

Higgins had enriched his life, and had planned to make an honest woman of her on his return, but as with many of his plans, he could easily get distracted.

'Edward, as you are so concerned about Katie's interests, I can assure you that it is my intention to do the right thing by her. However, that is for another day'.

Edward turned away, contemptuously sniffing the air. He turned to face Katie with a sceptical look.

'We'll soon see if this fellow was worth waiting for'.

As they made their way to the village, Robert caught sight of the first public house and suggested that a welcome home drink might well be in order.

Edward was scandalised at the suggestion.

'Have you forgotten that it's Lent, or have your new friends destroyed your faith completely?'

Robert resented this insensitive, if jocose, remark.

'Don't you start. There will be enough having a go at me without my brother joining in'.

Robert had forgotten all about Lent. Since he had been away, the weeks and months had merged into a meaningless pattern. Nevertheless, it was Saturday, April 13, just over a week away from Easter Sunday.

Katie feigned anger at the suggestion.

'I would not be caught dead in a pub during the holy days of Lent. God knows what class of women you have been dealing with for the last couple of years'.

The Liturgical Year was not something that Robert was particularly interested in.

'Lent! I'm afraid that slipped my mind completely. I still don't know what I will give up. Maybe I should give up sweets'.

He knew that his irreverence would annoy his brother.

'You could stop being a pain in the arse', Edward retorted.

Robert smiled his most annoying smile.

'No, that would not suit me at all. We all need to have a laugh and a joke'.

Robert quickly realised that he was in for a period of adjustment.

Robert's flippant remarks about Lent made her wonder whether his faith could have been a casualty of the war, although the same lad had never been scrupulous about matters of faith. In every aspect of life, Robert was more an individualist than a team player. He never saw himself as being part of a herd or congregation. His interest was more personal, preferring to worship at the altar of his own desires.

Waiting alongside the cart, Edward was growing impatient.

'Are we right so?

 Robert enquired whether Katie intended to accompany them on the cart.

'Do you think I'd be caught dead on that old yoke,' she teased.

'You two lads can do your sibling bonding. I have my bicycle with me'.

The brothers looked as if bonding was the last thing on their minds.

There was awkwardness to their relationship, and polite meaningful conversation between them was an unlikely prospect. The simple truth was that they embarrassed one another, both being happier when apart from the other.

As Katie was about to cycle home, Robert promised that he would call to her house later in the evening. Her sense of protocol dictated that she allow him spend his first night in the bosom of his family. After all, she was not part of the O' Connor family yet, but things were looking up. She had renewed confidence that her days as Miss Katie Higgins might be drawing to a happy end.

'Robert, you stay with your parents tonight, and we'll catch up after last Mass tomorrow'.

As Katie picked up some speed on her bicycle, Robert stood to attention at the front of the cart, and in a typically flamboyant gesture, he gave her a military salute.

'See you at noon down by the Abbey'.

Edward, alert to the sensitivities involved, was mortally embarrassed and checked to see if anyone was watching.

'Robert, you are not in the army', he snapped.

Robert laughed at the absurdity of it all.

'Show off'!' Katie thought, as she continued on her way.

It was ridiculous and immature, but secretly Katie loved it.

Chapter 3

Julia O' Connor was a woman of her time, resigned to a life of struggle. She was waiting at the half-door when she heard the sound of cartwheels on the flagstones. Bran, the old sheepdog, had alerted her that something was afoot, but like the rest of the household, he seemed unsure whether the wayward son should be welcomed or attacked. His mother had almost drowned him in Knock Holy Water when he left for the war. Now, the Holy Water was sprinkled again, this time in thanksgiving for his safe return. To Robert's eyes, his mother's hair looked much greyer than before and the dreaded rheumatism had tightened its grip on her.

Julia O' Connor lived for her children and loved them all, but the one she prayed for most was her youngest child, Robert. His selfish nature worried her. At times, she adored him, but there were also times when she could have strangled him. Perhaps, being the youngest, she had been more indulgent of him. Julia had little interest in the progress of the war or its causes. Her interests were entirely parochial. Adolf Hitler's death may have been important to many, but for her, it was nothing compared to the death of a neighbour.

'Blessed Virgin Mary, we will always be in your debt for bringing our son safely home'.

Robert had been away for too long. She was disappointed that he was not at home to celebrate her sixtieth and his father's sixty-fifth birthdays, but Robert had never celebrated their birthdays anyway. She smiled as she took her son into her arms once more.

Robert's sister, twenty-eight-year-old Norah, joined her mother on the front street.

She greeted her brother, and expressed her delight at his safe return. Norah was a pleasant and straight-talking girl with a sociable nature. Presently, delicate negotiations were being conducted to arrange her marriage to a respectable neighbour called Hughie Martin, a man fifteen years her senior. Norah did not have a problem with the age difference, and unsurprisingly Hughie had no issue with it either. Norah's expectations from romance were very practical and realistic. The depiction of romantic relationships on the screens of the *Gaiety* and *Savoy* cinemas in Sligo was merely the stuff of the imagination. In the real world, the ideal groom was a God-fearing man like her father, who was industrious and sober.

Despite never being a military or even a political activist, Tommy O' Connor belonged to the sentimental wing of Irish republicanism. The man was never likely to fire a shot in anger much less take a bullet for any political cause. Robert's father was a quiet and thoughtful man, who was not likely to get very excited about anything. He waited in the kitchen for his son to come to him. There was no point in running out to see him. After all, the young lad wasn't going anywhere soon. Nevertheless, he saw this as being a very special day. With his flat plaid cap pushed back carelessly from his balding forehead, Tommy got to his feet when his son darkened the doorway and extended the hand of friendship towards him.

'Leave it there, Robert. It's good to have you home. You caused a lot of trouble for us, but let bygones be bygones', he said, clutching his son's hand warmly. Robert scanned the room and found that precious little had changed since his departure. The dark wooden settle bed was still there, and the open dresser continued to display its burden of *Blue Willow* crockery.

The Sacred Heart picture still held pride of place, continuously lit by an oil-filled votive light.

During his absence, Robert had learned that, in a crazy world, such constancy could help preserve one's sanity by providing a sense of normality and security. The same could be said for the comforting aroma of homemade bread and freshly churned butter. This was a cocktail sufficiently potent to remind him of his childhood and reassure him that he really had made it safely home from the war. Tommy seemed pleased that his son had returned, but the fatted calf was never under serious threat. Edward had stood by his father in Robert's absence, so Tommy had no wish to antagonise him by making too much of a fuss over Robert. Nevertheless, he called for a drop of the hard stuff he had kept for this day.

Julia went to fetch the mugs from the dresser, but Tommy insisted that this was a special occasion.

'Not the mugs! Get the best glasses. I'm told that this is the best stuff produced in these parts for years. Now, fill up your glasses and drink to Robert's safe return'.

Julia protested that she could not drink the poteen.

'The last stuff you had nearly stripped the enamel off my teeth. If you don't mind, I will toast Robert's return with a drop of spring water'.

The four remaining glasses were filled.

Tommy proposed a toast.

'Here's to Robert's safe return. He may be a headstrong fool at times, but he is our headstrong fool and a brave one at that'.

Edward felt that Robert was getting a better reception than he deserved.

'It's good that Robert is alive and well, but let's not lose the run of ourselves. Don't forget he walked out on us in search of some excitement and went to serve the old enemy, alongside Protestant bigots from up the North'.

Tommy O' Connor objected to his son's portrayal of Protestants.

'Listen here, Edward, I will have no criticism of Protestants in this house. You and Robert are both called after Protestant patriots, Emmet and Fitzgerald. Do I have to remind you that it was Protestants who founded Irish republicanism in the first place?'

Tommy swallowed hard before he continued.

'Now that I have said my piece, you will not hear another word from me about your decision to wear the uniform of the Crown Forces. However, I think you will find that some of the neighbours might not be as easy to win over'.

Robert knew his father's direct style well and knew he was sincere. He smiled and raised a hand to acknowledge the sentiment.

There was no question, but he was relieved to be back where he belonged.

Once those formalities were over, Tommy chatted with his returning son. He made polite enquiries about the nature of his crossing from England.

'People tell me it can be very cold on the boat'.

He also remarked favourably on his son's physical appearance.

'The drilling seems to have given you a good shape. I hope they taught you some discipline somewhere along the way'.

'Not so much that you would notice', Robert smiled.

Edward was unimpressed at the small talk. He considered that his brother was a North Leitrim version of the Prodigal Son, a wayward country boy who tired of the mundane and sailed away to seek adventure and excitement. In his absence, Edward and his father slavishly farmed the unproductive thirty-acre holding of poor pastures and useless scrubland.

Four good acres of the meadow was the only redeeming feature. This meadow produced the winter fodder for the livestock. A vindictive spell of summer rain could well leave them in desperate straits.

Over tea, Julia filled Robert in on all recent newsworthy events in the district. Robert wasn't particularly interested, but politeness demanded that he pay respectful attention.

At her own pace, Julia updated him on all who had recently died, married, emigrated, and the one or two who had been sectioned in the Mental Hospital in Sligo. 'Timmy Dolan is still going out with Margaret Lynch. They started walking out together before we ever heard of that Hitler man, and yet there is no sign of them tying the knot yet. Long churning makes for bad butter'.

She reported how a neighbour girl, Marie Smith, had injudiciously struck up a relationship with a smooth-talking commercial traveller, only to become pregnant with his child. Julia was not unusual in viewing sex outside of marriage as being one of the more serious sins in the catalogue. Robert was more circumspect on the matter.

'I don' think it's any big deal at all'.

'Wash your mouth out', Julia snapped.

'You are getting to be like the people you served with'.

Over supper, Norah pushed her brother to describe some of her brother's wartime experiences. She had minimal interest in the details of fighting or logistics. She was curious about everyday matters, like the food, sleeping arrangements and how they passed the time when they were not fighting.

'And did ye all get a day off?'

Norah made it sound like the war was a nine-to-five business that left a day free for shopping.

'And would there be much storytelling or music at night?'

Robert looked at her in disbelief and snapped at her.

'We were fighting a war, Norah, not putting on a variety concert'.

In the household, there had developed a curiosity about how the respective relationships were progressing.

The conversation inevitably turned to Robert's plans for Katie Higgins.

'That girl will be looking for some commitment because she kept her end of the bargain', Norah predicted.

Robert rolled his eyes in exasperation, but Norah felt obliged to remind her brother of his responsibilities.

'You'd better think of marrying her soon because she has been asked to wait too long already'.

Robert appreciated that he could hardly drift back into his old life and just take up where he left off, but wished that people might let the subject lie.

He was already beginning to display the first signs of irritability.

'Give me a break! I haven't had a chance to piss since I came back and ye are already expecting me to map out my future'.

Norah heard him, but showed no sign of relenting.

'That girl was waiting around for you when many would have given up on you'.

'I'm glad to see Katie gets approval from everyone', he remarked.

In an attempt to shift the focus from him, Robert posed a provocative question.

'Who is the nicer girl, my Katie or his Alice?'

Edward turned his head in disdain, but before he could reply, his sister answered for them all.

'I can tell you Katie's the best you will ever get anyway, so make the most of it'.

Robert chose to turn the spotlight on his sister.

'What about yourself and Hughie Martin? Anything to report there?'

Norah gave him the latest update on the matter.

'I think there might be an arrangement soon'.

The girl described it as if it were some sort of business arrangement, the finer details of which still had to be finalised.

'Yea, we might be onto something there'.

Tommy agreed.

'Hughie is a very respectable man. Your sister would have a comfortable holding there. Fifty acres of quality land, the very best in the area'.

Norah basked in the reflected glow of this positive affirmation.

She was not an unattractive girl, yet her beauty could never have been her dowry.

Despite the level of discussion, it was not a made match in the traditional sense.

 She and Hughie had danced a few times in the hall before Lent brought an end to all entertainment. Certainly, the pair seemed to get on well together. In the past, Edward and Robert used to poke fun at Hughie, imitating his limp and slight speech impediment, but now it was time to show the man some respect.

Inevitably, the subject of Edward's ongoing relationship with Alice Kelly would be up for discussion. Edward reported that the relationship was progressing well, but there was unlikely to be any wedding bells in the near future.

'I'm waiting till I see how the ball hops'.

The vague nature of his response annoyed his brother.

'Edward, it's not a bloody football match. It's your plans for marriage'.

Despite this reticence, Edward must have been serious about Alice. In the past, he had dated several girls without ever even mentioning their names to his family. He only introduced Alice Kelly after they had announced their intention to marry.

This was an unusual engagement. There had been no trip to the jeweller's shop. He considered such expense as nothing more than meaningless show. Possibly, he may well have felt differently had he the price of a ring.

Whatever the position was, Alice seemed to have gone along with this without any real protest.

Tommy soon grew bored with all this talk of relationships and resurrected the topic of the war.

'Normandy must have been a scary time for you lot!'

'It sure was. We knew for a while that we would be making the crossing, but we did not know exactly when. It was scary,' he agreed.

His father was all attention as Robert filled in some of the details.

'We were three weeks in the camp waiting for the invasion. After that, they put us onto ships where we spent three nights being tossed around on the sea. We were supposed to head for one beach and then another. The sea was rougher than you could imagine. Hundreds of men died before we even hit the beaches'.

'God bless us and save us! Julia responded.

'It was prayer alone brought you safe'.

Robert was not a man to assuage his mother's fears.

'You know Mother, I often imagined that I would be coming home in a box, and ye would be digging a hole for me above in the Abbey'.

The very thought of that was enough to send Julia into convulsions of crying.

Her husband was less emotional.

'The prayers never go unheard', Tommy affirmed.

He continued to fill Robert in on farming life in the latter years of the Emergency. Robert had little or no interest in that, but good manners dictated that he feign interest.

When the topic of milk was raised, Robert was reminded of his former position in the creamery.

'I hear that little Murphy lad has my old job, or at least that's what he was crowing about when he saw me at the station'.

His father confirmed that this was the case.

'He has the job, the little bastard, and he'll be damn lucky to hold onto it because he's too lippy for his own good. A sparrow fart like him should be under the bed yet'.

Robert was disappointed but not surprised.

'I don't know where I'll get fixed up in a job'.

'Have you much money saved over the last couple of years?'

Robert answered rather sheepishly.

'Well, it was tough out there and you never knew when a bullet or shell with your name might come along and blow you into kingdom come'.

His father cut to the heart of the matter.

'So, you blew the lot', he said with disapproval in his tone.

His son had not changed at all.

'Joe Murphy might have a few hours in the yard on a Saturday if you get a chance to talk to him', Tommy suggested.

Then looking at Edward, he suggested that perhaps Alice might enquire whether anything was available, as she worked for Murphy. Edward reluctantly agreed to do so.

'I will, but I can't see why I should. This fellow blows a fortune and we have to help line up another job for him'.

'I understand, but it's only because he is family', Tommy replied.

The talk in the O' Connor house continued until about midnight when Tommy reached up to the mantelpiece and pulled down his set of rosary beads. Edward and Norah fumbled for their beads while Julia handed Robert a spare set.

'I'd say you have lost track of your own with that crowd you were hanging with'.

All five family members turned around and knelt, leaning into the wooden chairs and taking it in turn, to recite a decade of the Rosary. The others uttered the set responses.

Tommy did not content himself with the basic version of that traditional prayer. He added trimmings of his own. A recent addition was a prayer to God to secure a good husband for Norah. Tonight, there was a one -night-only prayer of thanks for Robert's safe return from the perils of war.

After the prayers were concluded, Tommy, in his nightly ritual, took down the clock from the mantelpiece. After winding it, he replaced it face down on the mantelpiece

'Half eight Mass in the morning for your mother and myself anyway', he reminded his family. I suppose Robert, you could do with a bit of a lie-in and tag along with Edward for last Mass at eleven'.

He stopped suddenly as he remembered something important. Without saying a word, he headed outside into the yard, returning a few moments later with a goodly portion of a fir tree in his arms.

'With all the fuss about Robert coming home, I nearly forgot about tomorrow being Palm Sunday'.

'Poor us', said Edward. 'We'll be weak from standing for the long gospel. Fr Maguire will drag it out to the last'.

Robert suggested bringing some sandwiches and a slice of apple tart with them.

Julia missed out on the sarcasm.

'Not if you are fasting for Holy Communion', she warned.

Julia considered it sinful to joke about religion or criticise God's anointed clergy.

'Stop mocking religion, will ye! It can only bring bad luck. You wouldn't complain about an extra few minutes at a football match. You should be on your knees, thanking God that you can stand for the long Gospel'.

'I'm sure that makes sense to someone', Robert laughed.

The good nights were said, and Robert took his candleholder and candle, which his mother had thoughtfully lit and took it upstairs with him. He was back in the same room he had occupied as a child. The room space was separated from Edward's room by a flimsy wooden partition. Not surprisingly, the acoustics left much to be desired.

Robert could hear every turn his brother made and every breath he took on the opposite side of the divide. Robert was worried that the poor acoustics might cause embarrassment for him. For the last few months, he had suffered from recurring nightmares, which threatened to disturb the peace of the household.

Once settled into the old camp bed, he surveyed his surroundings. The religious icons were all in place. It was like a football team lining out as selected. The *Child Jesus of Prague* looked innocently at him from across the room. *Martin de Porres* kept an eye from above, while *St. Teresa* covered his flanks. He was very well protected.

After a few moments, Robert blew out the candle and rested his eyes. The bed was warm. It was unlikely he would need the heavy overcoat to lend extra weight to the bedclothes.

As he tried to find sleep, the barking of dogs competed with the relentless soundtrack of war, which seemed to be running on a loop in his mind. He closed his eyes and attempted to clear his troubled mind. Yet, sleep proved to be elusive.

Nevertheless, he was so glad to be home.

Palm Sunday lay ahead. His suit would get another outing in the morning for Mass in the parish church. He would meet Katie Higgins again. Hopefully, they would go for a romantic stroll together and get reacquainted.

The world already seemed a brighter place.

Chapter 4

Sleep came to Robert only in short snatches. He lay awake for much of the night, fearful of reliving the recurring images that had disturbed so many of his nights. He was again haunted by the sight of his colleague, Norman Smith, his two legs mangled and lying in a pool of blood. Norman was screaming for help, and Robert was so woefully incapable of offering any. He had literally turned his back on his dying mate, unable to look at the horror.

Then, there was Reginald from Derry or Londonderry, as he insisted on calling it. Reggie took a bullet to the side of his head. He died on Sword Beach in Normandy. Robert desperately tried to focus on something less traumatic. He wanted to move on and leave those memories behind him. On the continent, the war was over. At night however, the war continued to rage in Robert O' Connor's bedroom in Dromahair. As a result of sheer exhaustion, he eventually nodded off to sleep.

He awoke with alarm to find himself drenched in a cold sweat, and found it difficult to go back to sleep. In less stressed moments of waking, he considered his future. He thought about Katie, and how she was entitled to evidence of commitment from him. Very soon, he intended to make that commitment.

His bleak employment prospects were another source of concern for him. A man needed a job to give him a degree of independence. He was not enamoured at the prospect of living back with his parents again. There was no progress in that. He needed to have an income of his own and a place of his own, and he needed to be more careful of his money in future. Unfortunately, his prospects were not looking good. While the military battles had ended, other battles loomed.

His mother's voice awakened him at half-past nine.

'I thought that all you soldier types got up at six in the morning', she joked.

'I could sleep for a week, Mother', he replied, rubbing his still weary eyes.

'It's great you had a good rest because the gospel this morning was fierce long. I had to sit down twice. Poor Mrs Mc Gowan had to be carried out of the church. She collapsed just as Pontius Pilate was washing his hands', she added by way of clarification.

'I hope the poor woman will be alright'.

His mother dismissively waved her hand.

'The same woman has form in that regard. You would think that she would have the sense to sit down'.

'Maybe she was afraid Pilate would crucify her too if she sat down', Robert joked.   His mother was not listening. She had her Sunday chores on her mind.

'I'll start peeling the spuds for the dinner while you get yourself cleaned up a bit'.

In Dromahair, First Mass at eight-thirty, was attended by parishioners who wished to receive Holy Communion and had therefore fasted from midnight. This early option was popular with the mothers of the parish. They would be home within an hour, and could make a start on the dinner while the others were at Second Mass.

The Sunday dinner was the highlight of the family day and the culinary high point of the week. As in most rural villages, a certain ritual was associated with Sunday Mass. Before and after Mass, a dozen or more men of various ages would stand, backs to the wall, on the opposite side of the street. These stalwarts of the Sabbath typically discussed cattle and crops as well as local and district news. It was a racing certainty that the first sight of Robert O' Connor was eagerly awaited. While many would privately condemn him, Robert knew that others would have no scruples about voicing their displeasure to his face. He was naturally quick-witted and was unlikely to allow any such remarks to go unchallenged. He liked to think the fascination with his return would be little more than a seven-day wonder.

Dressed in their best Sunday attire, the O'Connor brothers cycled together towards the village. There was little or no chat between them. As they dismounted their bicycles, the first person to approach was Josie Taylor, a middle-aged farmer and a distant relation of the O'Connor family. Having a natural curiosity about most things, Josie was especially fascinated with the rather toxic mix of guns and politics. The first time Robert ever held a gun was when Josie gave him his shotgun for rabbit shooting. Josie shook Robert warmly by the hand and was sincere in his welcome.

'You are very welcome back, Robert. I often thought of you when I heard about the German losses. I knew that you would let them have it. You will have to call in some evening soon for a long chat, that's if you can tear yourself away from Katie Higgins'.

Robert laughed. 'I will make time, Josie', and he meant it.

Inside the church, segregation of the sexes was the order of the day. Men occupied the seats on the right-hand side of the aisle and the women occupied seats to the left. The brothers took a seat near the back door. Edward was inclined to move higher up the church, but his brother was not to be persuaded.

'I fear I could get nose bleeds if I went up too high'.

The Mass was celebrated in Latin with only the priest and the altar boys with speaking roles. The congregation acted as the respectful and silent audience. As such, they were free to praise the Lord in other ways. Some read from their timeworn prayer books stuffed with inspirational material, memorial cards and even handwritten prayers. The Rosary and *The Memorare* were the prayers of choice of many worshippers.

The murmurings of prayer filled the air like a swarm of bees on the trail of spiritual nectar. Members of the congregation lovingly kissed relics of their favourite saints, some of whom had proved their worth in previous times of need. The well-practised routines of standing, kneeling and sitting were observed, depending on the relative solemnity of the moment. The sermon was, of course, delivered in English. This provided the priest with an opportunity to speak on the gospel or more likely in Fr Maguire's case, to address issues of concern in the parish. Today, there would be the extra ingredient in the form of the blessing of the palms. The priest would walk down the central aisle, sprinkling holy water on the palm-holding faithful in the body of the church. He would not forget the couple of dozen people on the gallery, many of them appearing to have season tickets for that elevated position.

While waiting for Mass to begin, Robert kept an eye out for the arrival of Katie Higgins. He did not have long to wait. The young girl entered the church, looking demure and self -conscious. Co-incidentally, colour co-ordinated for Lent, she sported a purple coat that he had often seen her wear. She, too, carried copious amounts of palm. Her fair hair was softly curled, and her sparkling eyes seemed focused only on the altar. Katie gave no indication of being aware of his presence although her romantic radar had immediately pinpointed his location. Robert may have been too distracted to notice, but he was also the focus of much attention. Edward was only too conscious of this, and was fearful lest he might be considered guilty by association.

Fr Maguire proceeded with his trademark, pedestrian pace. The long gospel proved to be an endurance test for many. The priest did not feel the need to tell the older and weaker individuals that they were permitted to sit if standing became too much for them. Therefore, it was inevitable that there would be casualties, as was the case at First Mass. On this occasion, two elderly ladies needed to be assisted from the church after slumping forward in their standing. Fr Maguire did not see any need to dispense with his usual Sunday homily. True to form, he detained the already impatient congregation for an additional fifteen minutes, offering his musings on how parishioners had observed Lent. He complimented those parishioners who had persevered with their Lenten sacrifices, and admonished some weaker spirits who had succumbed to the temptations of Satan. It seemed there would always be winners and losers in any activity.

After Mass, the congregation gratefully melted away to their bikes and carts. Robert strolled down to meet his girlfriend at the pre-arranged spot. He had advised his mother that he would not be home for dinner.

'And are you not eating at all?' Edward asked.

'If I'm good, Katie might let me have a nibble of something'.

Edward was not impressed by the suggestive nature of the response, but he let the remark pass.

Chapter 5

A few yards from the church stood the Abbey Hotel. Behind it lay a tree-lined pathway across the Bonet River leading to Creevelea Abbey, where the O'Connor dead lay buried. Even though the sun was shining, there was still a nip in the air. Robert and Katie parked up their bicycles before strolling arm in arm under a canopy of branches.

They took advantage of the isolation to talk with some degree of privacy. That privacy was short-lived as many locals walked that pathway as a shortcut on their way home from the church.

'O' Connor, you boyo! The Germans did little to change you', a former classmate good-naturedly shouted.

'Good to have you back in one piece, Robert'.

Robert acknowledged the greeting, but was not to be distracted from the beautiful girl by his side.

'Well, how does it feel to be back?' Katie asked.

'Bloody great, but it's a bit strange, I have to say'.

'What is it like to have me back?'

'Bloody great, but it's a bit strange', she comically echoed his reply. 'Seriously though, it's absolutely wonderful, and it's even better that you are back in time for the Easter Sunday dance. This year, it's to raise funds for repairs to the roof of the parochial house'.

'Oh, is the roof falling in on the good priest? I would have thought a religious man like that would love to view the heavens from his bed'.

'They say there's a fair bit of dry rot there'.

'I see, so we'll be dancing this night week,' he said.

Katie was delighted to be able to go to a dance with her man again. She hated such social occasions when she was alone, but her friends usually insisted on her joining them. They thought they were doing her a favour. At the dances, there were plenty of men showing an interest in her, but she had little interest in any of them. Robert was her man, and she remained faithful throughout his absence.

Predictably, she had to put up with some nuisances who sought to take advantage of Robert's absence. Pat Mc Manus was one of the more unsavoury predators. He had been in the same class as Robert in the local primary school, but that seemed to count for nothing. Pat had harassed her on many occasions.

The man could be obsessive and did not take rejection very well. His strategy was to raise doubts in her mind concerning Robert. 'You are naive if you think you and O' Connor can just take up where ye left off. War messes with a man's head. If I were you, I would look after my own interests'.

Avoiding Pat at those dances posed serious challenges for Katie. On occasions, she felt forced to seek refuge in the toilets. However, he always seemed to have a nose for her reappearance.

At the end of a set, he would be first in line to charge across the floor, and secure her as a partner for the next set. Even in the *Excuse Me* dance, he could be guaranteed to cut in on any of her dance partners.

While Pat may have viewed her as a free agent, most men saw her as Robert O' Connor's girl, and they did not want to get the wrong side of Robert.

Katie gained some small satisfaction in studiously ignoring him every time the *Ladies' Choice* dances were called.

Now that Robert had returned, she looked forward to triumphantly eyeballing him. That would put Pat in his place. She had, on occasions, toyed with the idea of telling Robert that Pat had made her social life a misery, but she feared Robert's reaction. She did not want any trouble, just an end to the man's pestering of her.

As the river flowed peacefully behind them, Katie and Robert were soon absorbed in each other's company. They held hands as they chatted, with Robert talking frankly about the war, the risks to his life. He had a greater fear of being maimed than being killed.

Not wanting to monopolise the conversation, he asked how Katie's job was going.

Bill and Wilma Carrington, an elderly English couple living in the old Church of Ireland rectory employed Katie to perform some light household duties. Their house was located at the end of a private road through a mile of woodland. The work there was light, but the pay was poor. Still, every pound helped.

Robert planned to call on his former employer in the creamery to enquire if any work was available. He would also check out the possibility of Saturday work in Murphy's Yard. Alice Kelly was willing to put in a good word for him.

Robert was intrigued to hear what people had been saying about him. Without naming names, she relayed some of the commentary on him. None of it came as any surprise to him. He knew that it was an unpopular career move that reflected badly on his family. Nevertheless, he entertained few regrets.

'Katie, I did the right thing. It did not please some, but that's their problem'.

Katie asked about how he fitted in with the Northern Protestant lads in his regiment.

'Not great! I was a papist bastard to them. I suppose they didn't know what to make of me. They probably thought that a Catholic lad from North Leitrim had to have a screw loose to join up with them.

Anyway, after some time, even the most unusual things get accepted as normal. In the end, I think they gave me a fool's pardon'.

'Did they really give you a rough time?'

Robert reflected on this before answering.

They certainly did at the start. A few of them were out and out bigots who would skin you in the blinking of an eye. But I didn't care about them shouting 'Fuck the Pope' or 'Burn all Fenian bastards'. It was all just noise coming at me. They soon got tired of shouting insults when they got no reaction. Now, I got into a fight with one or two of them, and I more than held my own in those fights. That showed them I was no pushover, and things improved gradually. They had to accept that I signed up for the same cause they did. Of course, when we went into battle, it didn't matter a damn who or what I was'.

'Were you able to make any real friends there?'

'I had only two real friends. One was a lad called Graham Patterson. We hit it off from the first days of training. Poor lad, he got killed immediately he jumped off the boat in Normandy'.

Katie could see that Robert's mind was drifting away from the peace of the old Franciscan abbey to the absolute hell on the beaches of Normandy. However, as his eyes showed signs of welling up, Robert was suddenly back in the moment. It was as if some unseen hypnotist had snapped his fingers and broken the spell.

'The other lad I was friendly with was Billy Parkes. He was a decent sort and managed to get me out of a scrape or two. I suppose I returned the favour on a couple of occasions. He's the only one of the bloody lot that I plan to keep in contact with. We swapped addresses, and we hope to meet up again'.

'I would love to meet him', Katie declared.

'He might fill me in on some of the things you got up to'.

'Jesus, we had no chance to be up to much. It was generally either fighting or sleeping, but you will probably meet him. He must feel he knows you from all the times I spoke about you'.

Katie was pleased to hear that he had spoken of her to his comrades. This nugget of information set her mind more at ease.

Katie suddenly became conscious of the time passing. It was after one o'clock, and her mother would have the dinner ready.

'Are you getting a bit peckish, or did the army train you how to go without?'

'Go without what, Kate?' he asked.

'Food, I mean, she emphasised. 'What else could I possibly mean?'

'You can rest assured that I am still a red-blooded male with an appetite for food and other things as well'.

'If you like, you can come over to our house for your dinner'.

'Thanks, Katie. I thought you would never ask'.

'Well, the cheek of you! Come on so, my mother has an old hen roasting, and there will be more than enough for everyone'.

Robert asked for her indulgence as he wished to visit the O' Connor family plot a few yards away.

Even though Katie was in a hurry home, she readily agreed to accompany him. Robert, being inclined to pray, was a novelty for her.

On nearing the family plot, Robert vaulted over the wall, before assisting her across the stile some yards further down. A couple of dozen steps then brought them to the O'Connor burial plot.

Robert looked rather nervous as he stood silently facing the headstone before picking a few weeds from the grave. It was terrible to think that Robert could be interred there now had circumstances taken a different twist.

'Robert, I have a question for you'.

'Shoot, as the officer said to the Private'.

'How real was the fear that you could be killed?'

He did not need any time to consider that question.

'It was real and it was always with me, but I don't want to think of that now because I have a question for you'.

'I'm listening', she responded, wondering where all this was leading.

Taking a deep breath and drawing himself up to his full height, Robert began to speak.

'Katie, how would you like to be buried here with my people?'

She was in no doubt as to what he meant and for a moment, Katie was rendered speechless.

'Are you asking me to marry you?' she eventually asked.

'I most certainly am, Miss Higgins, and I am waiting to hear your response'.

Katie emitted a squeal of delight and danced a few steps of her graveyard shuffle, before throwing herself into his embrace.

'Yes, I will marry you, as you knew well I would. Why do you think I waited for you all these months? Now, we have to do things properly. You will have to ask my father for my hand in marriage'.

'And I would want the rest of you thrown in as well', he stressed.

'And, Katie, I was thinking we might go into Sligo on Easter Tuesday to buy the engagement ring.'

Katie had to pinch herself to make sure that she was not dreaming. Arm in arm, they walked back the few yards to collect their bicycles and together make their way to the Higgins homestead. They met with several people on that journey, but Katie did not notice any of them. Her mind was elsewhere, thinking about what lay ahead. She could not contain her excitement. She even raced ahead of Robert on her bicycle, wrapped up in her happy thoughts. Her soon-to-be fiancé seemed to understand this, and he allowed her the space she needed.

Robert suddenly had to plan an approach to Gerry Higgins.

After rehearsing some possible lines and then forgetting them, he decided to improvise when he got there. As they were about to lift the latch on the front door, Katie had one piece of advice.

'Eat first; then I will get Ma and Joseph out of there'.

Chapter 6

Robert was quite familiar with the Higgins family, and had always been well received by them in the past. However, time had moved on and circumstances had changed.

He was hardly the ideal son-in-law. He had neither a job nor any immediate prospect of securing one. His standing among the community had taken a severe hit. All in all, he was far from what a respectable farmer would want for his beloved daughter.

Gerry Higgins was a balding, bespectacled man of stocky build with a relatively easy manner. He had a tendency to start most of his sentences with, 'Aye' or 'I see'.

This habit gave the misleading impression that he was playing for time, but it was nothing more than an ingrained habit. Gerry did not speak very much, but was a decent sort who liked to do the right thing by everybody.

His wife, Margaret was a more spirited creature. She did not tolerate fools, and told people exactly what she thought of them. Physically, she looked like an earlier edition of her daughter.

Katie had inherited her fair hair and baby blue eyes. Fortunately, she had not inherited her mother's quick temper. Margaret was a hard worker and a great manager of the family finances. For six or seven months of the year, she bartered eggs and vegetables for her other household purchases. In addition, her skill at dressmaking proved to be a nice little earner. Most of this work lay in making alterations to garments from clothing parcels sent to local families by relatives in America.

Gerry and Margaret had a second offspring, their son, Joseph, who was now a twenty-year-old and worked the farm with his father. Sadly, Joseph had a rather unsightly, purple birthmark on his cheek. This blemish made him very self-conscious. Fortunately, he was now able to grow facial hair that promised to hide much of that embarrassing mark.

Joseph liked to hunt and play pitch and toss with neighbours at the crossroads, but he was a quiet type that would never annoy one with talk.

Margaret was setting the table, oblivious to what was about to unfold. When the door opened, she began to speak before she looked at who was there.

'We were about to go ahead without you. Joseph and your father had their tongues out for a bite to eat'.

Robert was to her heels, and his presence brought a momentary halt to the conversation.

'Well, the Devil arose and appeared to many', Margaret blurted out. 'Katie told us you were back'.

Gerry got to his feet immediately, and extended a friendly, yet unenthusiastic, hand.

'Good to see you're still in one piece anyway'.

'Thanks, Gerry, I suppose all my mother's prayers had to have some effect'.

'There were plenty more maybe calling down curses on you', Margaret responded.

'I am sure you are right', Robert conceded.

'Anyway, I'm glad the prayers worked, and I lived to tell the tale'.

'Did you kill any Nazis?' Joseph was impatient to know.

'I certainly shot at a fair few of them, and some went down. But I couldn't say whether any died or not'.

Joseph was fascinated.

'Did they go down roaring?'

'Well, there was so much noise around you that you would not hear yourself thinking'.

'Have you any German helmets home with you?

'I didn't even bring my own helmet back, much less a German one. I'm not into collecting trophies or reminders. Anyway, I need no reminders of that time'.

'Do you even have your gun home with you?' Joseph naively asked.

'Are you joking me? I don't think the British government would be daft enough to let me loose in this state, with one of their weapons'.

Joseph's mother interrupted his line of questioning.

'I presume Katie invited you for a bit of dinner', Margaret's tone betrayed her lack of enthusiasm at the invitation.

'Yea, Mrs Higgins, she did. She told me you had a big bruiser of a hen roasting in the oven'.

'I have indeed. Now, you go and sit down there, for there's plenty of meat on the bird'.

'Are you fussy about the colour of the meat?'

'What?

'Do you prefer the leg or the breast'? Margaret snapped impatiently.

Robert looked at an embarrassed Katie, who offered just a hint of a smile.

'Beggars can't be choosers. Throw me any scrap, and I'll eat it'.

Katie hurried about, getting crockery and cutlery into place. Gerry took a mug and plunged it deep into a shiny new bucket of spring water that sat on a stool near the door. He invited Robert to do the same.

'I need the drop of water with my dinner, or else it repeats on me. It must be too dry for my system'.

The steaming hot potatoes were placed on a large plate in the middle of the table alongside a jug of fresh milk. Gerry had tidied away a copy of the *Sunday Messenger*, which he had just been reading.

Katie's brother, Joseph, furiously started peeling potatoes, fearing the hungry guest might reduce his quota. However, there seemed to be an ample supply for everyone. The potatoes were slightly over-boiled, but that did not bother any of them.

Gerry said the grace and finished with his customary line.

'The ball is in, and the game is on'.

That line had nearly become part of the grace by this stage.

A few moments of embarrassing silence forced Robert to take on the role of conversation maker. There were further moments of awkward silences, which Robert felt obliged to fill.

'How do you think Leitrim will fare in the football this year? Have they a chance in Connacht?

'Aye. I suppose it will be the usual hard luck story, unless they get the boys back from England, and that's not too likely. They will get it tough to muster a team at all'.

'They might come looking for me'. Robert joked.

Gerry looked straight into his face.

'Well, maybe the Brits will testify that, at least, you can shoot straight'.

Robert interpreted this as a feeble attempt at humour from the older man and not as a slight on him. Still, he was much too nervous to crack a smile.

'Who do you tip for the Connacht title?' Robert asked.

'Aye, there's a tough question now. I think it could be Roscommon, but who knows? Isn't it fifteen against fifteen when they get out on that pitch?'

There was no arguing with that.

Over dinner, mother and daughter chatted about the people they had seen at Mass and who was home for the weekend. Today, their conversation was embarrassingly stilted. The arrangement was that after dinner, Katie would take her mother out of the kitchen on some pretence or other and leave the coast clear for Robert's little chat with Gerry. There was no problem getting her mother away from the men, but she had to be more imaginative with Joseph. She told him that she had heard a car coming along the road. Since the war and petrol rationing, cars on their stretch of road were as scarce as hens' teeth.

Once on his own with his prospective father-in-law, Robert decided to dispense with the small talk and cut straight to the chase.

'Gerry, I am here on a mission. I want to marry your daughter. I am here today looking for your permission and your blessing'.

Now that the question had been asked, Robert felt some relief.

It was now Gerry's turn to feel under pressure.

He had been taken by surprise and seemed dumbfounded for a few moments.

'Aye.'

His expression offered no indication of his feelings.

Robert felt the need to keep talking as the heavy silence bothered him.

'Katie is a great girl, and I think a lot of her. I hope she thinks a lot about me too'.

'Aye, she always looked out for the postman bringing your letters, even though she knew the half of it would be censored anyway'.

The conversation ran into another awkward silence.

Gerry wasn't making matters easy, but this was unintentional on his part.

Robert was again forced to push his case.

'I would look after her. You know that?'

'I do, aye, I do. I think you are well-intentioned, but you don't have a job or an income, do you?'

Robert feared that his lack of finances could prove a sticking point. Maybe he was foolish to push his case so soon. Perhaps he should have had a wage packet or two before proposing marriage. As of now, he was not exactly a great catch. He had no land, no job, no income and few prospects.

'To be fair now, I'm just back from the war. There's a chance of some work very soon. Joseph Murphy seemingly has Saturday work in the yard, and I'm checking out the creamery tomorrow. They might have a few hours too'.

'So, have you nothing saved from your army days?'

Robert had to confess that he had not managed to save anything. This admission was not likely to enhance his standing with the patriarch of the Higgins clan. He couldn't argue with Gerry when he said that one needed more than a 'live horse and you will get grass' approach to life.

Their chat was not going as well as Robert had hoped it might. He recognised that he had presumed too much. Still, Katie had not anticipated that there would have been much of an issue with her father. Her mother might well be a different story.

Gerry finally broke the silence.

'My preference has always been to leave decisions about my daughter's future to the girl herself. I know she thinks you are the cat's pyjamas. Maybe she is right. You might not have a penny to your name, but I feel that you would look after her and treat her well. If she wants to marry you, I will not stand in her way'.

Robert breathed a sigh of relief and reached over to shake Gerry's hand.

'Thank you, Gerry, you won't regret this'.

'I hope not, Robert. I hope not. Now, if the two women would come back here, we could drink to your health'.

Margaret had been made aware of the situation in the kitchen. She was not pleased at the prospect of her daughter marrying the unemployed man. Furthermore, she had reservations about his personality.

'That lad is too strong-willed for my liking'.

'But, I truly love him, Mother'.

Margaret threw her head back.

'Listen to the voice of innocence. Love won't boil the pot. What do you intend to live on, fresh air, is it?'

Katie knew that she would have said the same things had their positions been reversed. She could be accused of being innocent, but she knew Robert, and she knew that he was not shy of hard work. If anything, he could be overly concerned about making money.

'You can come back in now', was the message to the women.

Gerry knew Katie well enough to know that she had already acquainted her mother with the nature of the business at hand.

'I think we are losing a daughter, or are we gaining a son? I wonder.' Margaret put her view on the record for Robert.

'It seems our daughter wants to marry you. I still have doubts about you, but I am willing to set them aside. I hope that you will do your best to look out for her. If you don't, you will have to deal with me. Having said that, we won't withhold our blessing. We wish you well, but don't expect her father or me to be dancing with joy about it.'

That was enough for the happy couple and enough for Gerry to produce a drop of the hard stuff to mark the occasion, if not to celebrate it.

Chapter 7

There was no part-time work available at the creamery. The manager seemed pleased to see Robert again, and promised to give him first refusal on the next vacancy. Young Jimmy Murphy wore a smug expression as Robert walked past him.

He had guessed the reason for his predecessor's visit.

'You should never have given the job up'.

Robert had to draw on every ounce of his patience to resist the temptation to give him a wallop, but that would be counterproductive. Instead, he opted to ignore him and leave the young lad talking to himself.

Very soon, another Murphy came up trumps for Robert. Joseph Murphy in the General Merchant's store agreed to employ Robert for Saturday work in the yard. This involved delivering heavy and bulky purchases on a horse and cart. As often is the case, one man's misfortune is another man's opportunity. The longest-serving employee in Murphy's Yard, Paddy Mc Loughlin, had suffered a fractured shoulder following a heavy fall from the delivery cart. The incident seemed innocuous, but the injuries sustained were likely to prevent Paddy from returning to work any time soon. Paddy was in his sixties, and this did not bode well for his return. An injury to the arms or shoulders is a major handicap when doing such heavy work. The upshot was that Robert was given an additional three and a half days of work. Tuesday would be his day off. As with all other retail outlets in the village, the business would close for a half-day on Wednesday. The payment was at the rate of fourteen shillings a week. It wasn't great, but it was a start.

When they heard the good news, Robert's parents were not surprised that a second family wedding was on the horizon. The wonder was that Katie had waited so long for him. Tommy wondered what the living arrangements might be.

'Where do you plan to live when you're married because I have nothing to offer you here?'

This sounded harsh, but Edward was already considering converting the barn for Alice and himself, although he seemed in no hurry to give them a day out.

Julia had no problem with her son's choice of wife. She liked Katie, but didn't want to share a kitchen with her.

'She is a decent girl who cycles to Mass every Sunday and does the Stations of the Cross before Confessions on Saturday morning'.

Robert would be willing to help out on the farm when needed, but he accepted Edward was the heir apparent to Tommy. He was interested in the land, and unlike Robert, he never abandoned his parents.

One evening, the two brothers chatted as they moved cattle from one pasture to another. Edward, who was being unusually civil, asked about the likely timing of the wedding. Robert hinted that his engagement might be quite a long one, as he needed money to rent a house and keep Katie in some degree of comfort. He would need an extra few bob and wondered if Edward had any ideas.

'There's feck all money to be made around here. Anyway, you are asking the wrong man. What do I know about anything outside of the farm?'

'You would be more in the know that I would. Anyway, where there is a will, there's a way'.

'Maybe you are right, Edward, but you are not exactly blazing a trail to the altar yourself, and you have a place to live. Do you realise how lucky you are?'

Edward's expression was not that of a man who felt gratitude for his circumstances.

He liked the farm, but knew that he would never make a great living from farming. The only consolation was that he would always have the little plot to grow potatoes and keep a few hens and cattle. There was a certain security in that, but the commencement of reconstruction work on the barn was not a priority.

Despite his brother's disinclination to engage in discussion, Robert persisted. He told him that he had always said he would marry Katie once the war was over. He realised that he had no God-given right to have his woman wait indefinitely for him, but thankfully, she had waited.

'And how do you know you are the man for her?' Edward asked.

The question was not one he had been expecting. It forced Robert to attempt to articulate his intuitive position.

'I think she's keen on me. She's missed me something awful. Even her family told me that. While I might have messed around with others, I have always been true to Katie'.

'But how do you really know that she is the one? And these other girls you dated, were you thinking about them too, while you were away?

Robert was puzzled by the intensity of his brother's cross-questioning. His looks were scarily severe.

'Well, now Edward, a priest, in confession might ask me that but not my brother'.

'But, how do you know that there's not another man out there who can make Katie happier than you can or can make Alice a better husband than I can?'

Robert slapped his brother on the back.

'You can never know for certain, and if you wait until you're certain, you will never do anything. There are few certainties in this world'.

Edward nodded an unwilling agreement on this point, at least.

'I suppose you are right about something for once', he ventured.

Chapter 8

With the end of Lent, there was a great sense of release. An end had
been reached for the black sugarless tea, the countless rosaries and
the closure of dancehalls that greatly impacted younger people.
Now, these dance halls could reopen their doors. On Easter Sunday,
the singletons of the parish could take to the dance floor again.
The hall was quite small, holding no more than three hundred
people. The procedure was the same all over the country. The single
ladies positioned themselves at one side of the hall and the
unattached gentlemen on the other side, with sort of a demilitarised
zone between them. The yielding floorboards emitted the wonderful
smell of the wax. Overhead the spinning silver moon rotated, giving
the drab building a rather sophisticated vibe. The mineral bar was
well stocked to quench the thirst of the most energetic dancers. The
atmosphere was one of eager anticipation as the doors were thrown
open to the revellers.
Edward and Alice arrived at the hall with Robert and Katie.
For some moments, the couples continued to converse while
observing other patrons queue up at the door to part with the
admission charge. As monies raised were going towards the cost of
work on the roof of the parochial house, Fr Maguire was likely to
make his appearance later. This priest was a rather formal and aloof
figure. Despite his facility for small talk, he seemed uncomfortable
on such social occasions.
Typically, at such fundraising events, he would arrive at the hall at
about ten o'clock. The band of local musicians would finish their set,
and the priest would then address the assembled patrons.

He would thank them for their support and urge them to be generous. After that, he would then take his leave and retire to his bed for the night. Unlike many of his contemporaries, this cleric did not patrol outside the hall, dissuading any amorous couples with intimacy on their mind. He hoped that his sermons had clearly communicated the church's position on such matters.

When the dance floor was sufficiently populated, Robert led Katie in a familiar foxtrot around the floor. He was not a technically adept dancer, but he displayed such an energetic and flamboyant style that it seldom failed to attract attention. On the other hand, Edward was one of the most nimble-footed dancers in the hall. He danced waltzes, foxtrots and quick steps as fluently as he swung a scythe in the meadows.

It was a night on which Katie could strut her stuff with the love of her life by her side. She danced every set, and had not to endure interference from Pat Mc Manus. He had caught her eye earlier in the night, while he was leaning against a sidewall, his eyes fixed on her and her beau. Katie luxuriated in the quiet satisfaction in being able to look her former tormentor in the eye and not be fearful of him.

At the end of each set, there was an almighty surge of men towards the ladies' side. On occasions, this force threatened to drive some unfortunate females through the sidewall. Invariably, some girls were in greater demand than others, and some men found it difficult to get a dance partner.

After an hour or so into the dancing, there was an overwhelming smell of perspiration in the air. Like Robert, many men had dressed in their best Sunday suits with shirts buttoned tightly up. Most girls used the opportunity to show off the very best of their finery. Many of these gorgeous outfits were homemade as material was still scarce and expensive.

Many of the settled couples took an occasional breather from the dancing to sit at the far side of the hall and converse or just observe the dancers on the floor.

Unsuccessful suitors looked sheepish and embarrassed, as some associates jeered at them or worse still, looked piteously upon them. There was a practice known as the 'duty' dance among the better-reared boys. Mothers might have instructed them to give certain neighbour girls a dance. These boys were under instructions to look out for any wallflower and give her a whirl on the floor. This outing on the floor could provide a kick-start that might generate more dances for the recipient.

The hall's policy was that a girl should not refuse a request to dance unless the man displayed signs of intoxication or was, in some other way, offensive. In practice, however, the girls were free to pick and choose their partners if they were fortunate enough to be in demand. As the night wore on, there was the usual loud guffawing, accompanied by backslapping by nervous young men to give the impression of being at ease.

This was far from the truth as all men risked rejection every time they crossed the floor. Handshakes and friendly nods were afforded to returning locals. Stories of what it was like in the North or in England vied for attention with talk of the deplorable price of cattle and the poor prospects of a good Connacht championship for the county.

Surprisingly, there would be a scattering of older men in the hall. These veterans of previous dance hall campaigns had long since hung up their dancing shoes. They were mostly bachelors, and while they were no longer actively seeking a wife, they still liked to observe the next generation going through their paces.

While Robert was catching up with people he had not seen in some time, and Edward danced with girls from the area, Katie and Alice chatted amiably. They had so much in common, being roughly the same age and both having outgoing personalities. Besides, both girls seemed destined to marry an O' Connor man. Alice was a beautiful girl, taller than average, with raven black hair, which she wore shoulder length. The girl had wonderfully expressive eyes.

'It's great you and Robert are getting engaged, but I hope the engagement won't be as long as ours. And I hope you get a ring to show for it'.

'What do you think Edward is waiting for? Is it doing up the barn or getting a few pounds or what?'

'I haven't a clue. Edward says there's no rush, but time moves on. A girl wants to have her bargains made. Sometimes I feel a bit anxious. I would love to be married and experience the thrills of being man and wife, if you know what I mean'.

Katie knew well what she meant.

'Yea, I suppose, but until that wedding band is on my finger, I will be fighting Robert off with a stick if I have to. Men never respect you for doing otherwise', she claimed.

Alice smiled ruefully.

They compared notes on the brothers and laughed at the idiosyncrasies of both.

Edward was much more sensitive than Robert. He had a much greater sense of duty and responsibility. Recently, he seemed more introspective and slightly more irritable. Recently, Robert and he always seemed to spark off each other.

'I hear that Tuesday is the big day, Katie. Choosing the ring and all that?'

'Yes, it is Edward and I can't wait to be Mrs O' Connor.'

'Mrs O' Connor, that has a nice sound to it,' he conceded.

'How do you put up with him?' he enquired.

'Well, it's like everything else, I suppose. You get used to him. Seriously though, I really think that we are soul mates. I think we are made for each other'.

'I think it's great that you can say that, to be so certain', he mused.

Katie felt that she needed to pay Alice a compliment.

'You are a lucky man too with Alice. She thinks the world of you. You know we could even have a double wedding yet, Robert and Alice and you and me'.

Katie laughed at her unfortunate mistake.

Edward smiled along with her.

'Stranger things happen, I suppose'.

'No, I don't think so'.

'So, when will you and Alice be settling down, do you think?'

'It depends. There are a few things that I am sorting out. We will let things settle'.

'Don't leave it too long, Edward'.

'You need not worry there. I know a good woman when I see one.'

They were interrupted by an announcement from the stage.

The bandleader had called the start of the 'Lady's Choice' set.

Katie returned to claim Robert, and Edward returned to Alice. The floorboards yielded perfectly as the dancing feet traipsed merrily across the crowded floor. It had been a great night. At the very end, the band struck up the national anthem. Everyone stood to attention. The most erect and perhaps the most respectful during the anthem was Robert O' Connor, who was hearing the anthem for the first time since he left the country.

Despite his years in the service of another country, he was Irish and proud. He was still a single man, but that was soon to change. The love of his life stood alongside him. He would willingly surrender his unattached status on Tuesday.

Chapter 9

Work in Joseph Murphy's Yard involved fetching bulky, pre-paid items for customers and securing the dockets for book keeping purposes. Occasionally, there was a considerable amount of heavy lifting involved. Saturday afternoons generally saw Robert on home deliveries. He enjoyed getting away from the work place.

Robert was the only staff member not to work in the shop itself so most of his social interaction was with customers. Yet, he enjoyed the banter with Alice, his prospective sister-in-law, who worked in the kitchen.

The proprietor, Joseph Murphy was a middle-aged man who had inherited the business from his father. As a youngster, Joseph was in a privileged minority of locals whose family could afford secondary school education. He was a decent sort and enjoyed a reputation for fairness and generosity. However, he was nobody's fool. While he permitted trusted customers to run up credit in the store, these individuals were good bets to pay their bills over the medium term, when they recovered from their temporary difficulties.

Joseph Murphy was also an undertaker and had once operated the post office. He read the newspaper each day and liked to update his customers on the latest news from home and abroad. While Robert made himself available for any overtime that might become available, there was precious little on offer. After being away for so long, his biggest challenge was in adapting to home life again.

His mother did not demand rent from him, but he willingly contributed to household expenses and helped out on the farm when it suited him. Nevertheless, he longed for his own place and true independence.

Even though his parents didn't make many demands on him, they still insisted that he be present for the family Rosary each night. Robert had already missed the nightly prayers twice in the first week. This did little to endear him to the other family members. 'Remember Fr Peyton's words - 'The family that prays together, stays together', his father quoted.

The parish priest felt that many younger people were not sufficiently serious about their religious practice.

Tommy O' Connor agreed with his parish priest on that point and was looking forward to the upcoming Mission, which Fr Maguire had organised. Hopefully, this exercise in spiritual renewal would re-energise the faithful.

Following the recommendations of clerical colleagues, the parish priest had secured the services of two formidable Redemptorist priests. These two men were booked for the third week in June and a sense of anticipation was already growing in the parish. Such events brought their own drama and excitement. Meanwhile, on the home front, Norah could soon be flying the coop. An autumn wedding was definitely on the cards, with September being the favoured date.

The delicate but smooth negotiations with Hughie Martin were progressing well. There was talk of Tommy selling a couple of heifers, with the money going towards Norah's dowry. While Hughie and Norah got on well together, Hughie still insisted on some form of sweetener before he would close the deal. He farmed some of the best land for miles around. This asset, he considered, should count for something extra.

He also had an uncle in the priesthood, which enhanced his status considerably. The O' Connors had no problem parting with a lump sum because it would be their own daughter who would be spending it.

When Hughie called into Murphy's Yard for some supplies, the prospective groom was particularly civil towards Robert.

'I need two pounds of staples for a fencing job on a field I plan to keep for meadow'.

He pronounced each syllable of each word as if he was trying to impress a hard-of-hearing elocution teacher. Still, he was a decent sort, and Robert had no worries about his sister's welfare after she married him.

He had no worries either about Alice Kelly being good for Edward. Alice was such fun that Robert wondered what she was doing with his brother. Apart from her infectious good humour and lively personality, the girl was really attractive. He enjoyed her company and liked to think that she felt comfortable with him too. He wondered if she would have been interested in him, had the circumstances been different.

Robert considered that he had mellowed somewhat since his return to civilian life. Edward did not annoy him as much as he had done, and he seemed to have generally developed a greater tolerance of fools. Maybe the war had accounted for some improvement in his character. However, there were other legacies from the war that were extremely negative in nature.

Robert's sleep continued to be disturbed by recurring nightmares. Fortunately, he had only awakened his brother on one occasion with his shouting. In response, Edward had burst into his room wielding a broom handle he had grabbed in a hurry.

'In the name of God, what on earth is wrong with you? I thought some mad man had broken into the house and stuck you with a pitchfork'.

Bathed in cold sweat, Robert angrily muttered that it was just a nightmare. Edward left, shaking his head in annoyance and disbelief. 'Some brave soldier you must have been'.

'I should have known not to expect sympathy from you, Edward.'

'There is very little sympathy for a man that brought his trouble on himself'.

'At least, I had the sense to go away and sample life in other places'. Edward scoffed at the very notion.

'From what I gathered, it was death you sampled. The real living was done here while you were ducking and diving with your Northern friends'.

Chapter 10

Easter Tuesday turned out to be a busy day in Sligo town. The spring
sunshine lightened the mood of all, as they went about their business
along the narrow streets of the market town. Robert and Katie
attracted little attention as they stepped off the train and set about the
happy business of getting engaged.

On this red letter day, Robert was giving his army issue suit yet
another outing.   Katie had taken great time getting herself ready for
this very special trip. She was unsure what to wear but finally settled
on the red floral pattern frock she had altered last summer. It had
been a cast-off from a wealthier and taller cousin in Philadelphia
who had worn it on graduating from High School. As she linked
arms with the man of her dreams, Katie was the happiest girl in Sligo
town that sunny morning. If ever there was an occasion to wear a
bright, sunny outfit, this was it.

Katie's aspect had taken on a new radiance. Arm in arm, she walked
from the station, in the direction of O' Connell Street. Her
excitement grew as she entered *Wehrlys* jewellery shop. The
gentleman behind the counter welcomed his two nervous customers
and warmly congratulated them on the happy occasion.

Robert, mindful of his limited budget, had rehearsed an introductory
sentence.

'Don't let the suit fool you into thinking that I am a schoolmaster or a
bank clerk. I am just back from the war and I have little to show for
it'.

As it happened, he did not need to use that line. Being practised at determining a customer's station in life, the jeweller correctly guessed the man's means and concentrated on his less expensive range.

Katie took her time and tried on ten or more rings. She tried each one with the excitement of a child let loose in a sweet shop. One was more appealing than the other. How could a girl be expected to choose?

Robert was ill at ease in this situation, and he would have preferred to wait next door in *Hargadon's* public house until Katie had made her choice. However, it was Katie's day, and he was determined to be as gentlemanly as he could.

However, Robert began to perspire again as the more expensive rings in the cheaper tray still were too pricey for his limited budget. Apart from his own possible discomfort, he wanted to spare Katie any embarrassment resulting from his lack of funds. After some time and more delightful agonising, Katie had finally come to a decision. She chose a beautiful solitaire ring.

'Robert, you have made me the happiest woman in the whole country today'.

'You can keep me company so, as I am the happiest man in Ireland right now'.

The owner smiled at their interaction as he processed the payment. The outer blue case displaying the retailer's name was similar to ring boxes she had previously seen in Mrs Carrington's jewellery drawer.

Katie would even treasure the box. It would never be thrown out or even used to hold anything else. Robert knew that today's date would be forever etched on Katie's mind. She would treasure that ring, and furthermore, she would bequeath it to her eldest daughter if God blessed their marriage with a family.

After leaving the jewellery shop, the nearby Sligo Cathedral was her first port of call. She and Robert walked up the short distance to Sligo's Catholic Cathedral, where she lit two candles and knelt in front of the main altar. She uttered an earnest prayer of thanksgiving, not just for her engagement but also for Robert's safe return from the war. There was much to be grateful for.

As Robert had an early breakfast, he was already feeling quite peckish. Katie suggested that they return to O'Connell Street and dine in the *Ritz Cafe*. She had been there with her mother on one previous occasion and liked its ambience. Robert was not bothered where he ate. For an hour or so, Katie took in her surroundings and pretended that dining out in restaurants was a regular feature in her life.

As it was Easter, Katie opted for the hot cross buns and tea for two. Unlike Robert, she could well have passed the entire day without any food at all. Her thoughts were on higher things. For her, Love was its own nourishment, but the man of her dreams tucked into both buns, licking his lips with satisfaction afterwards. Katie enjoyed the sit-down, and while Robert ate, she took time to replay every detail of the magical day thus far.

'Don't you wish things could stay like this forever?' Katie asked.

Robert smiled, but he was already tired of wandering the streets, dressed up like a solicitor's clerk. The next SLNCR train would be departing soon, and he would be glad to get back to Dromahair and change into his everyday garb.

Katie had different ideas. Leaving the *Ritz Cafe* she spied the Rosses Point bus pulling up across the street, and before Robert could say 'Home', he was crossing Hyde Bridge and on his way to The Point. He graciously accepted that it would be the late train for him.

Looking at Katie he could see that she was savouring every moment of the day. Despite his rising boredom levels, it would be a pity to rush her. She was entitled to her day out and he had nothing urgent to attend to anyway.

He needed to relax and make the most of the day. Rosses Point was thronged with people taking advantage of the Easter sunshine. Katie wanted to walk along the promenade first and then dip her feet in the sea. Katie linked her arms in Robert's as they sauntered along, gazing into the broad Atlantic. There was also a crowd playing golf on the course there, which had attracted a lot of attention. Ahead of them, the sight of Coney Island in Sligo Bay captured her attention. 'Robert, wouldn't it be so romantic if we lived in one of those little houses on the island? Think of the peace we would have, looking out on this beautiful scene, knowing that all the fuss and the noise in the world would not invade our little space'.

Such romantic thoughts fell on barren ground where Robert was concerned.

Isolation held little appeal for him. The man thrived on companionship, and reducing his social contacts was not advisable.

However, this was not the day to be contentious.

'It would be a long walk to Murphy's Yard in the mornings. I don't think there is a direct bus from Coney to Dromahair', he replied.

After enjoying an ice cream and a bag of sweets, Robert's impatience returned and he could not wait get on that train again. Katie was in no such hurry. She had yet more pleasure to extract from the place, but luckily for Robert, there was a definite chill coming in from the sea. For the first time, Katie was beginning to feel cold in her light dress.

It was time to take the bus back into town.

It had been the happiest day of Katie's life. She had filed away all the mental images she would cherish for as long as she drew breath. Despite his occasional moments of impatience with Katie's slow approach, Robert was glad that Katie had enjoyed the day. Feeling bored for a few hours was a small price to pay when he considered how faithfully Katie Higgins had waited for him.

He had given Katie something that meant a great deal to her. She had a ring on her finger. Hopefully, the pressure would be off him for some time.

Chapter 11

Margaret Higgins may not have been enamoured with her daughter's choice of husband but she readily understood what it meant for Katie. The first stop for the newly engaged couple was her parents' house.

Margaret certainly marked the landmark occasion. She dusted down the kitchen and scrubbed the floor. She even dressed in her best finery, and coaxed her husband into donning his Sunday suit.

When the newly engaged couple walked in through the front door, even the old sheepdog, Bran, seemed excited. The kettle had just boiled, and the aroma of fresh baking scented the air. It was easy for Margaret to time their arrival, as she knew the train timetable by heart. She rushed forward to greet her beaming daughter and pulled her close.

'I am so happy that you are happy, Katie. That is all I ever wanted for you'. Gerry contented himself with a handshake to his prospective son-in-law and a congratulatory slap on the back.

After mother and daughter separated, Margaret also extended a handshake to Robert but stopped short of kissing him, even though he had prematurely inclined his cheek to hers.

Gerry produced a bottle of *Tullamore Dew,* but the two ladies contented themselves with a sweet sherry. Margaret used a cloth to wipe the glasses clean.

'To Katie and Robert', toasted Gerry. May they live long and fight little'.

Despite the rationing and the resultant re-using of tealeaves, the brew was made good and strong as befitted the occasion. There was brown bread, fresh from the oven to go with the lettuce, cold meat and tomatoes, the standard fare for such an auspicious occasion.

Gerry felt moved to play music. He took down his fiddle and played a few reels and jigs accompanied by the unlikely sound of his wife playing the spoons on her lap.

'I never realised I was getting into a musical family. None of us can play a tune or hold a note', Robert admitted.

Gerry modestly explained that he was just a journeyman at the fiddle. His grandfather had been a great player.

'I'm not great at all, but sure I couldn't miss it. Aye, I suppose it is true to say that there was always a tune in this house'.

Margaret was interested in hearing the details of their day in Sligo. Katie was only too glad to oblige, recounting every detail in strict chronological order. She had recorded every moment of her experience from the number of people feeding the swans on the Garavogue River to the number of people in the train carriage on the homeward trip.

Margaret tried the ring for size, but her fingers were too thin to secure the ring.

'God help me, I had fingers like you once, but the hard work wore them down'.

Gerry didn't feel the need to hold the ring, but the two women were so insistent that he felt obliged to play along.

'Aye, that's a fine diamond. If we are ever stuck, we can use that for cutting a pane of glass.'

'No day arranged yet, I suppose?' Margaret wondered.

'No, it's a bit soon yet', Katie answered.

'Or where ye might be living afterwards?' Margaret continued.

'All in good time', Robert replied as the women withdrew to the scullery.

'Where's Joseph?' Katie asked.

'He's over with old Mrs Gallagher. She has a heifer that's expected to calve, and the woman was nervous on her own'.

Katie continued to fill her mother in on even the most minuscule aspects of the day.

Alone together, Gerry moved to throw another sod of turf on the fire. He took down his pipe, slowly and thoughtfully lit it before emitting a relaxing:

'Aye, ye had good weather too, by all accounts'.

'None better', Robert assured him.

'Were there many people around Sligo?'

'Loads of them, the Easter, I suppose'.

'Aye'.

In the scullery the conversation was going thirteen to the dozen, but words were at a premium in the kitchen. Yet, neither seemed to mind.

After the men's forays into such areas as the long-range weather forecast, *Old Moore's* predictions and even the progeny of local bulls, the females returned to the menfolk. Robert counted down the moments until he could plausibly take his leave.

Katie's big regret was that she had to remove her ring so often. She wouldn't wear it in her cleaning job in the big house as it might result in loss or damage to the ring.

Alice entered the general spirit of excitement. She did not have a ring herself and would have liked to own one. Of course, Edward had a different view. He claimed they could use the money more wisely.

'Plenty of women have no engagement rings and they get on without one,' Edward had stated.

Katie encouraged her fiancé to rent a property after they got married. Alice had heard something about Murphy's cottage down by the river, being available to rent. She had heard something about some man changing his mind on renting it. That would be a nice quiet spot. It would not be anyone's ideal location for a home as it was on the edge of the graveyard. Robert listened but was not inclined to do anything about a wedding or renting a property until he felt more secure financially. His position in the yard, badly paid as it might be, was just covering for poor Paddy Mc Loughlin.

That man could return at any time, even though the last report was that Paddy was hardly able to get out of bed. For Robert, the prospect of being a married man in such uncertain circumstances was not something he wished to countenance.

Margaret suspected that Robert viewed the engagement as a temporary sop to her daughter. Although it was an earnest indication of the man's commitment to her, she suspected that he might drag his feet on setting a date for the wedding.

Her daughter had no such reservations.

Long engagements were never seen as a great idea. There were endless stories of girls who had wasted their childbearing years on a man who shied away from commitment. The church was equally disapproving. The fear was that a couple might view themselves as being almost married and prematurely embrace the intimacy of that state. There was a lot at stake in the area of relationships and uncertainty was the enemy. Robert, for his part, was inclined to let matters settle for a while.

Chapter 12

Fr. Maguire liked to see himself as a man of the people. Thus, he sought to visit each house in the parish at least once a year. These pastoral visits also extended to commercial premises regardless of their religious affiliation. On the day of his visit to Murphy's emporium, the occasion was observed by the proprietor as something on a par with a state visit.

While on the premises, the priest could not help but notice the recently returned soldier. While Fr Maguire had reservations about Robert's decision, he decided to be magnanimous.

'Robert, I hear congratulations are in order. You are lucky to have a fine girl like Katie Higgins as your intended'.

Robert thanked him for the compliment and assured him that he was well aware of the lady's virtues. An embarrassing silence ensued, and Robert was at a loss as to what he might say next. He was very pleased and relieved to see Joseph Murphy deal with the gap in conversation.

The priest listened as Mr Murphy recited Robert's praises.

'He is a hard-working employee who is very punctual and gets on well with customers and staff'.

Robert considered this sounded more like an extract from a written reference than an impromptu remark about an employee. He wondered whether Murphy had already drafted a reference for him or the man was just making polite conversation.

The priest listened but did not comment. Instead, he returned to the subject of Katie's virtues. It was as if Mr Murphy had not spoken at all.

'Yes, Katie is a good girl who nurtures her faith and would never put it at risk'.

Robert could only interpret the remark as an implicit criticism of his past behaviour.

It was evident that the priest considered that Katie could have done better for herself.

'And I hope that, unlike your older brother, you are not going to keep the young lady waiting for her big day. In my experience, long engagements can be the prelude to ruination'.

Fr Maguire may have been slow at saying Mass, but he was far from slow in getting a dig in.

The proprietor listened respectfully to the rather lop-sided exchange and volunteered what he considered quite an interesting nugget of information.

'*The London Times* reported that Robert's regiment was the only one to feature both as an air force and land force during the Normandy Landings'.

The priest looked at Mr Murphy and then at Robert, wondering why Mr Murphy considered this worthy of mentioning.

He politely nodded to register appreciation of that particular fact before taking his leave of Robert's company.

'I don't want to be keeping you from your work Robert so I will take my leave and remember you have a fine girl in Katie Higgins. Don't disappoint her or me,' he added with menace in his tone.

Robert was left in no doubt that the priest and wider community believed that he was getting the better end of the bargain in marrying Katie Higgins. They were probably right.

Chapter 13

Robert's engagement seemed to spur Edward into action. He considered getting a price on the barn conversion, so that it might comfortably serve as a home after his wedding. While he did not seem particularly enthusiastic, Alice was pleased that matters were progressing.

A couple of weeks later, Robert and Edward were chatting in the kitchen of their homestead in the early hours of the morning. They had both been at Kitty Devaney's wake. Tommy had attended also, but he had gone to his bed by midnight. As usual, the alcohol was flowing freely at the wake and each story told surpassed the previous one. By three in the morning, the two brothers were back home, slumped into fireside chairs and lacking even the energy to walk to their respective bedrooms.

After rooting through his pockets, Robert retrieved a letter that had been delivered to him eighteen hours earlier by Paddy the Postman. Edward may have been intoxicated, but his powers of observation were intact.

'Is that an English postmark?' Edward enquired.

'It is an English postmark, and that's because it was posted in London, England'.

'You don't say. Maybe it's from the army. They might be looking for the suit back', he joked.

Robert took a moment to scan the contents of the letter.

'No, I'm stuck with the suit, I'm afraid. Anyway, it's not from the army at all. It's from a friend of mine who served in the same regiment. Do you remember me telling you about Billy Parkes?'

Edward nodded. He had heard a few names but had never really passed much heed of what were strangers' names.

'Well, Billy Parkes is over in London, working on the buildings and doing very well'.

The Luftwaffe had levelled many of the English cities.

Reconstruction was likely to be big business.

'Billy can line a job up for me if I am interested. His cousin is a sub-contractor there'.

Edward was surprised at the offer.

'Did you not tell him that you have a job in Murphy's and you just got engaged to be married?'

Robert did not see these as having any bearing on the issue.

'The job in Murphy's is only while Paddy is out. He could be back in a couple of weeks, and where does that leave me?'

Edward was sure that the job would be more long term.

'Paddy isn't even able to straighten up in the chair. There's no chance of that man being able to lift anything heavier than a mug of tea for the foreseeable future'.

'Maybe, but you can't bank on that. In England, there is serious money to be made on the buildings now. And with overtime on offer, a man could build up a nice nest egg pretty fast'.

Edward did not doubt this. It would be a great idea if a man were single.

'Yea, but you are engaged to be married. What would you want, leaving a good woman behind to go and live in a strange city where you would know nobody?'

Robert viewed life differently.

'I would consider it because we could save enough to get a small house or a bit of land, and wouldn't that be a great start to married life?'

Edward was struggling to absorb the import of what he was hearing. In his opinion, Robert should be down on his knees thanking God that Katie had agreed to marry him. Considering leaving her again to go chasing crocks of gold at the end of the rainbow was nothing short of madness.

Edward was shocked.

'Robert, you are stone mad, and I'm sure Katie will tell you the same. You can never be content with what you have. You always have to take risks to get something else. You had money before and you blew it. What makes you think that you would save some this time?'

Robert was annoyed by his brother's rather intemperate reaction and regretted confiding in him.

Long after the two boys eventually retired for what remained of the night, the brothers reflected on what they had discussed.

Robert dreamed of his returning from London, laden down with bags of money and being able to buy a little farm outside of the village. In his room, Edward imagined a scenario more favourable to himself. He dreamed of Robert foolishly outlining his insane proposal to a shocked and distraught Katie who had already waited so long for his return from the war. It might have only been wishful thinking, but it gave Edward some hope. Maybe, there was no great rush in working on the barn. This game had a little time to run yet.

Chapter 14

The first Thursday of every month was Fair Day in the village.

Katie loved fair days, but she particularly loved this one on June 6 1946.

She viewed the day as something of a metaphor for her own life. The dark days of winter had passed. Her markets were being made, and altogether there was a great sense of anticipation, with much to look forward to.

From early in the morning, the streets of the village were alive with people and livestock. Mobile food stands were in position to serve teas, soup and sandwiches to hungry farmers and cattle dealers. Oilskins and wellingtons were on sale for those who understood that summer did not mark an end to the rainy weather.

Katie's father had several lambs for sale. He and Joseph had arrived early and secured a good spot on Main Street, near the Garda Barracks. Her mother had a few hens for sale as well as a young rooster. There could only be one servicing rooster in any yard, and old Red Henry was not ready to relinquish his crown yet, so the young pretender had to find another yard in which to strut his stuff.

Edward was in the market for a young bull calf. Recent births on the farm had seen a run of heifers, so a young bull was needed for future servicing of the heifers.

There was a certain ritual evident where cattle sales were concerned. Cattle dealers strutted around in their trademark yellow boots, carrying ash plants as they meandered through the packed streets searching for bargains. These men were shrewd judges of animals but also of the farmers. Haggling was the order of the day.

When a buyer and seller came close to a deal, a third party might intervene and urge them to split the difference. When agreement was reached, the parties slapped hands to signify the deed. Many of the deals were then celebrated over a glass of porter in the nearest bar. As there were so many people in town, Robert was busy in the yard all day. The fair was a godsend for the merchants and publicans. It was a mini Christmas with a whole load of cattle dung thrown in for good measure. As the village had no fair green, the main street fulfilled this role. This necessitated the erection of barriers to prevent excited cattle from damaging the plate glass of the shop fronts. In the main, these were planks of wood nailed across empty tar barrels. Once Henry, the young rooster, and his female companions had been sold off, Katie and her mother were free to sample the day's pleasures. They decided to treat themselves to a scone and tea in one of the villager's front rooms, which transformed into an eating house for such days.

The Higgins ladies sat with their backs to the door, facing a wall featuring a street scene from pre-war Paris. Having their backs to the world allowed mother and daughter chat together without interruption in a pleasant environment.

Robert had agreed to meet Katie down by the mill as soon as the yard closed for business. In a rare trip along the road to sentimentality, Margaret wondered what the long-term future might hold for Katie. Might she find herself in the village on a fair day, enjoying a quiet moment with her own daughter?

Katie, encouraged by her mother's sentimental imaginings, asked Margaret how she felt after meeting Gerry for the first time.

Her mother was uncomfortable answering personal question, but she willingly answered that one.

'Oh, your dad was lovely. He had the finest head of curls, jet-black hair, and beautiful white teeth.

'Most likely, he brushed them with soot'.

Margaret laughed.

'Yea, the soot generally did the business'.

Katie was keen to probe a little more as she wondered what qualities her mother had sought in a prospective husband. She had already known what he looked like from old photographs.

Margaret shifted uncomfortably on the bare wooden chair and marshalled her thoughts before speaking.

'Well, he needed to be a practising Catholic to start with. And there was no way I would have put up with a heavy drinker', she continued.

'But apart from those things, was there anything about him that you were attracted to?'

'Well, he could make me laugh even if that was only because he started so many sentences with 'Aye'.

'Was he doing that back then as well?'

'Aye', he was', Margaret responded.

The two women's laughter filled the room.

Katie loved her man. She felt an attraction to Robert, and it had nothing to do with his religious faith or the waves in his hair. It was more about physical chemistry. She wondered if there had been that spark between her parents back in the day.

'Mammy, when Daddy courted you and took you out on the bar of his bike, did you feel any sort of attraction to him, physically, I mean?'

Margaret did not like the way this conversation was going.

'Now, girl, there was none of that sort of stuff in our day'.

Katie had to explain that she merely enquired about the presence of a spark between them.

'Sparks can be dangerous, and I'm not talking about around hay or in the woods in the summer time. The sparks, you are talking about, ruined many a life and reputation. And don't you forget that you are only engaged yet. You have no licence to be up to any sort of funny stuff. There can be many a slip between the cup and the lip'.

Katie had got more than she had bargained for. However, as the subject of sex had been already broached, there was nothing to be lost by digging a little deeper.

'I wasn't talking about sex before marriage or the like, as you know. I'm asking because I'm not sure what a woman does in those situations, if you know what I mean'.

Her mother's anger was assuaged as she began to see this as an understandable concern on her daughter's part.

'Listen, Katie, the man does what nature drives him to do, and you do what nature requires you to do. You have seen the bull and the cows in the field or the rooster and the hens. Don't forget this is all to procreate, and you have to remember that children are a blessing.

I hope God blesses you with children, but you can't maintain a whole army of them. You will know when to call a halt, and as they used to say in my mother's day- 'It's time to send him to sleep in the loft then'.

 Katie wondered why women were presumed to have no sexual appetite and why sex was seen as being just for conception. She felt she had a strong sex drive, and might have considered herself a freak had Alice not told her that she shared the same desire.

Margaret's generation of women did not consider such topics to be a fit subject for discussion. Margaret abruptly steered the conversation to the small matter of the wedding.

'Well, have ye any date in mind yet? We don't want long engagements, do we?

Katie was spared from answering by an over-eager waiter, who unceremoniously removed their empty crockery from in front of them.

'I am very sorry ladies, but if you are finished, we need the table. There is a long queue outside'.

The women gathered their possessions and vacated the premises.

Chapter 15

As Robert made his way through what remained of the fair, he was in the company of his work colleague, Alice Kelly. Both of them were on the way to meet Edward, eager to see if he had made a purchase.

Edward was nowhere to be seen, but a neighbour informed them that he had indeed purchased a young bull earlier in the day. It was unclear whether he had brought the animal home or got someone to mind it while he adjourned to one of the heaving public houses. Alcohol did not agree with Edward. Under its influence, he could become quite aggressive. Fearing the worst, the two of them started to check his more likely haunts.

There was no sign of him in any of those houses. That meant he was either gone home or, more likely, he had adjourned to the hotel bar. Edward was eventually discovered, drinking porter in the corner of the hotel bar. It was extremely noisy in there and people had to shout in order to be heard. His drinking buddy was none other than his neighbour and family friend, Josie Taylor. Josie was unlikely to lead Edward astray.

As Robert fought his way through the bar, a random man shouted abuse at him.

'Get out of Dromahair. We want no British soldiers here. There was enough of your sort here twenty-five years ago'.

Robert did not recognise the drunken loud mouth. He felt sure that the man had been set up to mouth the abuse by some embittered local.

Before Robert could challenge the stranger, some peace-loving drinkers had eased him away from his tormentor.

A local man, Charlie Jackson cautioned Robert on the dangers of provoking a potentially violent situation.

'Forget him, Robert. He's not worth it. He doesn't even know you. Some smart boy here has it in for you'.

A barman escorted Robert's tormentor from the premises, and a potentially explosive situation had been defused.

'You can't expect much else after you did the dirt on your country', Edward sourly remarked. His speech was badly slurred and his eyes looked dead in his head, but he was far from being unconscious.

Robert was concerned that Alice was outside waiting on Edward. He had no desire to upset her unnecessarily. He didn't know whether to send Edward out to her or send Alice away until his brother had sobered up.

Josie suggested that they should all go outside for a breath of air. Unfortunately, Alice was standing near the door of the hotel bar and saw the intoxicated state of her boyfriend.

'Edward O' Connor, you are a total disgrace to yourself and your family. How can I send you home to Julia in this condition? Come on, we'll take a walk down the street, and hopefully, the air might do you good.'

Before they left, Josie bought a tomato juice for Edward to drink. 'That should help', he remarked.

Alice fed him the tomato juice as one might feed a baby.

After she took Edward away, Josie and Robert continued up the main street.

'Why did you not get him out of there earlier?' Robert asked.

Josie explained that he had just arrived on the scene.

'Your brother had been there since he bought the animal at eleven o'clock in the morning'.

That came as a surprise to Robert.

'I wonder what he did with the bull calf.'

Josie was not worried on that score.

'I'm sure he had taken care of that first. He may like a drink on a fair day but he is no man's fool'.

Josie reported that as he arrived, the bar manager was urging Edward to call it a day and go home.

'I told them that I would handle the situation, so I went in and sat with him. I felt that something was eating at him, and I wanted to get that out of him. He opened up then and started on about you and how you ruined things for him'.

'You mean, all that war stuff'?'

'Yea, but you could have predicted that taking the King's Shilling would land you in trouble. People remember what the 'Tans' did around here. I remember them dragging my aged grandfather out of his deathbed to check for guns and hitting him across the head when they found nothing'.

'I know all that, but Edward seemed to have got over that, and we were getting on fairly well'.

Robert's going to war was not the only issue concerning Edward.

'I know, but he said you mentioned heading across the water for some job. That was annoying him big style'.

'Why the hell should he be bothered? It's no skin off his nose, is it?'

Josie paused before he replied.

'I get the impression that he thinks you are messing that Higgins girl about', Josie reckoned.

Robert was annoyed. If Edward had been telling Josie about London, he was probably telling others, Alice included. The last thing he wanted was for Katie to hear this from anyone other than him.

Robert took his leave of Josie and walked in the direction of the mill, his meeting point with Katie. He hoped that no one else got to her before he did.

Nobody had come near the girl as she sat near the millwheel, quietly sifting through her thoughts as the world went about its business.

As he approached, Katie saw him and rose to walk towards him. She gave him a gentle peck on the cheek.

'You look as if you had a hard day', she commented.

'Mad busy! By the way, did your mother get rid of young Henry?'

'Yea, Henry and his girls have gone to a new home together. Isn't it very exciting for them?'

Grabbing hold of his arm, she steered him back up the hill towards the village.

Anxious to have a quiet word with her, Robert sat her down on the low wall overlooking the River Bonet as it bade farewell to the village and wended its way towards Lough Gill.

'The river looks very brown this evening', Katie observed.

'Yea, it picked up a tan with all the sun we've been having lately', he joked.

'Or maybe all of the dung from the street today', she suggested.

Robert was tempted to philosophise about the progress of rivers, but decided that the time was ripe to allow her in on his thoughts.

'Katie, you know this yard job is only temporary, don't you?'

That came as no surprise to her. She was grateful that he had the job to keep him in the locality.

'I know Robert, but God is good, and if he closes one door, sure, he might open another. He brought you home safe from the war, after all'.

The reminder of those dangerous days still haunted Katie.

Robert was keen to get to the point, and explained that Paddy McLoughlin could show up in a few weeks or months and reclaim his position.

'Yes, and we will cross that bridge when we come to it'.

Robert tried another tack.

'Even if he never returned, the wage I'm paid is fierce small anyway'.

None of this was helping Robert's cause.

Katie adopted the attitude that God will provide.

Robert had little alternative but to come straight out with his news.

'Katie, I got a letter from my old comrade, Billy Parkes. He tells me that he's making great money on the buildings in London. They are re-building all that was bombed during the war'.

'Yea, good for him', she replied, puzzled as to how this concerned her.

'Yea, he said he's got work for the next few years if he wants it'.

Katie wondered whether there was a point to all of this.

'Does he want a medal for it or a round of applause or what?'

'No, Katie, that's not it. He just thought I might be interested in joining him there'.

'Well, I suppose it's good to know he's doing well for himself. Has he found a nice girl for himself yet?'

Robert was becoming frustrated that she had missed the full import of what he was saying. He suspected that she was not really listening to him at all.

'He didn't mention anything about a girlfriend, but knowing him, he wouldn't be short of a woman. He wanted me know that work was available in London if I wanted. He'd set me up in a job'.

Katie suddenly realised that Robert was about to suggest something that was an anathema to her.

The letter had evidently unsettled Robert. He was keen to join his friend there and was essentially asking her for her blessing.

Katie couldn't believe that her recently engaged man could consider leaving her again.

She stood up and looked into his eyes.

'Robert, you can't be telling me that you would take yourself off and abandon me again, only weeks after your homecoming'.

It was clear that Katie was upset and very disappointed in him.

He attempted to convince her of the merits of the arrangement.

'Katie, you are looking at this the wrong way. I want us to spend the rest of our lives together, but I don't want us to be scrimping and saving all of our lives. I can't provide for us properly on the few bob from Murphy's, especially in a job where I am only covering for a man on sick leave'.

Katie's eyes began to well up. This man had just come back into her life. He had proposed marriage to her, and already he was planning to leave her.

She was so upset at Robert that she turned her back on him. If the situation were reversed, she would have preferred to live on bread and water and be with him than leave him. He enumerated all the reasons why he should travel to London in search of big money.

'Katie, this time next year, I could be back here with enough money in the butt of my pocket to buy a small farm or a pub or some other business. We could be comfortable. We could have a great base to start a family'.

Katie lost the struggle to control her tears, and they came flooding out. She could feel herself shaking with disappointment. This was not the way she had envisaged things happening.

After a few moments her feelings of shock began to give way to feelings of anger.

'Robert, why do you want to leave me again? Why can't you stay at home and fight the battles here? Why do you always have to run like a coward away from responsibility?'

Robert was horrified by her reaction, especially at her use of the word 'coward'. Since his return, he had been called many things, but never had anyone termed him a coward.

'How is that cowardly?' he asked with a look of injured pride.

When no answer came, he put the same question to her for a second time.

'How can going to England to earn money to support you be seen as cowardly?' he queried.

'If you were not a coward, you would stay here and fight. You would fight against poverty and hardship, and you could succeed. You would fight to keep me happy. If you stay, we could be happy together, no matter how little money we might have. You cannot put a price on that', she cried.

Robert was unconvinced by what she was saying.

'You deserve better, and I deserve better. I would not have to hang around a merchant's yard every day, talking about the weather to anyone who steps into the yard. The job bores the arse off me. I could tolerate that if it were constant work but Katie, there is no guarantee of that'.

Katie snapped at him that life offered no guarantees and accused Robert of selfishness.

'Was the ring intended only to buy some time? A fancy ring is of little use when I might need a hug or a kiss or a sense of someone being there for me'.

Robert could understand that but insisted that a year was a relatively short time in their young lives.

'This could be the making of us, Katie'.

Katie was too upset and too angry to engage him in further argument.

'I want to go home, and I want to go home alone', she insisted.

Robert nodded his assent.

'But promise me one thing, Katie, that you will think about it'.

Katie did not reply.

She turned around and turned towards the village.

'Remember Katie, this is all for you. I love you, Katie and only want the best for you'.

Chapter 16

As soon as Katie walked in her front door, Margaret could tell that something was wrong. She sat her daughter down while Gerry stood over her, looking for some explanation. After a few moments of sigh-filled exclamations, Katie filled her parents in on Robert's plans.

Gerry was totally disgusted.

'The blackguard! Has that man no understanding at all?'

Katie tearfully explained that Robert claimed it was all for her.

Margaret had grave misgivings on that point.

She suspected that selfishness lay at the root of everything he did.

'It is not for your sake. That over-grown child is just bored by having to live back at home. He's probably just short on excitement. This place can be quiet after the excitement of war'.

'Aye,' Gerry joined in support.

'This place must be a bit dead for him, but he seems the unsettled type anyway. By the way, did he ask you to go to London with him?'

Katie explained that thus far, he had merely asked her to consider the prospect of his emigrating for just one year and coming back laden down with money.

'If that fellow goes away, he will not return', Margaret predicted.

'If you are not enough to keep him here in the first place, you won't be enough to bring him back', she continued.

It was difficult to argue with her mother's logic

Her father's comment on his being an unsettled type registered alarmingly with her. Even if he went and came back in a year, he might always see England as offering an out. It was bad enough now, but what would it be like if she had a few children to mind as well?

She reminded herself that he had already returned to her after the war but was she the big draw?

'Maybe, he was returning to the only base he knew. After all, where else could he go?'

Katie was again forced to consider whether Robert really loved her at all. These thoughts soon re-awakened the dark, negative feelings she had experienced during the war years.

Yet, Katie loved Robert O'Connor with her whole heart and soul. She did not want to risk losing the man of her dreams. In years to come, might she look back and see him as the one she had allowed to slip away? She could never forgive herself if that eventuality came to pass. She had waited for several years before and wondered whether she should wait for just one more. Maybe Robert would agree to stay but forever resent her for denying him a better life. There were difficult decisions to be made, and she felt weighed down by the task.

A couple of hours earlier, her foot had been light, and her heart even lighter. She had enjoyed a wonderful day at the fair, and had been looking enthusiastically towards their future together.

Now, she felt like a giant, multicoloured balloon floating gracefully over the ocean before it encountered unexpected difficulties. The air was escaping from that balloon and, with it, the hope and optimism from her body.

Many, including her parents, had argued that she had been foolish to wait for this man in the first instance. They had argued that he had displayed little loyalty to her or to his country and that he was motivated only by a selfish sense of adventure. Up to now, she had never felt so inclined to agree with them. Perhaps, her eyes were being opened to what she should have seen earlier.

Long after retiring that night, she lay awake, listening to the wind and the rain beating down on the corrugated iron roof, her mind convulsing with decisions and revisions. By three o'clock in the morning, she had settled on a response.

A short distance away, Robert O' Connor was still agonising over his future.

He was sorry that he had not followed Alice Kelly's advice. She had told him to put London out of his mind completely.

Alice and he had become close friends. She was a rock of common sense and he usually respected her opinion. Furthermore, Alice told him that he would be foolish to risk losing Katie. She insisted that he had a duty to settle down and act like an adult with responsibilities. However, Robert felt he knew best, and pushed the case for London. Alice also reminded him that Katie was a girl who had faithfully waited over thirty months for him, when she didn't know whether he would be coming back alive or in a box.

Robert understood, but he had put his own twist on that argument.

'Surely the girl could wait nine or twelve months more with the guarantee that he would be returning with money to secure their future'.

Alice had given her opinion, but Robert chose to ignore it.

Arriving home, deflated by Katie's reaction, Robert had to face the sight of his brother sprawled across the settle bed, nursing a hangover. Edward looked almost as bad as Robert felt after a tongue lashing from his mother. His drunken behaviour had shamed the family name.

Despite Edward's drunken state, he was determined to deflect blame by reminding her that he was not the son who had besmirched the family name.

'You and your British army friends, it was you who brought disgrace on us'.

Tommy called for an end to such discord.

He appealed to both sons to calm down out of respect for their mother and the sanctity of the family home.

'There was never any fighting under this roof, and I will not stand for any fighting now'.

His words were almost lost in the heated exchange between the brothers.

Tommy was horrified and astounded by what was taking place.

The entity that was the O'Connor family seemed to be crumbling before his eyes.

'Has my whole family taken leave of their senses? What the hell is behind this bad feeling? I thought we had put all that business behind us. Even the combatants have moved on. Why can't you boys?'

Tommy was adamant that there had to be more to Edward's behaviour than met the eye. He presumed that it could be attributed to sibling jealousy over inheritance or women.

'If I didn't know ye better, I'd say it was over a woman, but whatever the hell is the cause of it, it will be settled once and for all. I will not have two sons of mine upsetting the atmosphere in my house.'

'Did he tell you he's chasing off to England again to one of his Orange buddies? Did he?' Edward demanded to know.

Julia was dumbfounded. Tommy was able to articulate a response.

'Surely, you can't be serious, Robert. Are you telling me that you are taking to the road again after a few weeks at home? What sort of rolling stone are you? If you only knew how many novenas it took for your mother to get you safely home and you to consider breaking her heart again'.

Robert was too tired and too angry to deal with this.

Edward was on his feet, angrily waving his accusatory finger at his brother.

'What do you think Katie will make of her selfish fiancé, contracting to marry her and then running off like a scared rabbit?'

Even to Robert, his reasons for going were already beginning to sound hollow.

He attempted to further compose himself by taking a deep breath and counting slowly to ten. He felt sorely tempted to lash out at his brother, but he would have lost his dignity and brought heartbreak to both of his parents.

Instead, he contented himself with saying that Katie would take time to consider his proposal. Robert looked around. He saw nothing but angry and disappointed faces.

There was no family rosary recited in the O' Connor house that night, and everyone felt guilty for that.

Chapter 17

Saturday evening was never a good time to visit a country house, what with the Saturday evening bathing of children, the scrubbing of floors and the general preparations for the Sabbath. Nevertheless, Robert felt that he needed to speak with Katie as soon as possible. The terrible uncertainty of it was bad for all involved.

Katie knew his schedule, so she expected to see his bicycle make its way along the boreen sometime before seven o'clock. He finished work at six, and she felt he would be keen to talk to her soon after that. She felt great unease about what the future might hold for her, but she knew that she was no longer in the business of waiting. Robert was either going to marry her or leave her.

The reality was as stark as that.

Katie had been out pulling carrots for Sunday's dinner when she saw Robert approach. Unseen by him, she made her way inside. She took a moment to touch up her hair and generally check her appearance in the looking glass.

Joseph was still working in the fields while Gerry sat by the fire, feeling a little unwell. Margaret was heating the iron in the fire before getting to work on her husband's best shirt for Sunday Mass. Katie begged her mother not to show any animosity towards Robert. While her father was never likely to be nasty anyway, Katie decided that it might be best to bring Robert on a short walk, well away from the house.

Robert arrived at the door with a little less welcome for himself than was usual. There was little of the bonhomie or cheer, but he was courteous and gracious.

'Hello, Mrs Higgins, I'm sorry to disturb you on a Saturday evening, but I need to have a word with Katie'.

'You had better come in so', she answered without any warmth in her voice.

'How are you keeping, Gerry?'

Robert asked, ever anxious to maintain the social niceties.

'Aye, I'm alright apart from a touch of heartburn'.

'You should ask the chemist to make up a bottle for that'.

'I'll see if Katie is down in her room', Margaret said as she excused herself. Katie appeared and joined Robert on a walk down the winding laneway and onto the narrow country road.

Despite recognising that it might have been a mistake to raise the issue in the first place, Robert was already having a change of heart.

'Katie, have you thought about what I suggested?'

'About getting married, you mean?' she sarcastically asked.

'About going to work on the buildings in London for a year at most, something that really would set us up. Don't you agree?'

Katie took a deep breath.

She knew what she would say, and had rehearsed every word about a dozen times.

On this occasion, she was determined to deliver them as rehearsed.

'Robert, I know that your suggestion could be seen as an example of good, old-fashioned common sense, but our situation is very different to most'.

Robert sought to interrupt, but she immediately held her hand up for him to stop, as imperiously as any policeman at a checkpoint.

'No, Robert, let me finish. Our situation is different because I have already waited years for you. I waited, not knowing whether you would come home alive or dead'.

She could feel emotion welling inside her as she recalled those painful and worry-filled days.

'I did not know whether you would still want me, but I waited faithfully for your return. Just as I am beginning to breathe a bit more freely, you tell me that you are thinking of heading off again. Now, I have done my thinking.

I am telling you here and now that I am done with waiting. I have done enough waiting for two lifetimes. You have to decide whether you go to London or not.

My position is that if you leave me again, that's us finished. I won't be waiting anymore'.

Katie breathed a sigh of relief when she finished the last sentence. She was glad that she had the strength to utter all of it and the memory to recall each line. Now came the part that she dreaded. She had no control over what Robert was going to say, no power to influence his words or even her own response.

Robert looked shell-shocked.

He had retained a hope that Katie would come around and see the wisdom of his proposal.

He put his hand to his head and turned a full circle on the narrow road. He had not anticipated that response. After a moment or two of agitated silence, he pulled with a downward motion along his facial stubble, searching in vain for some sense in all this confused thinking.

A neighbour cycled past on a bicycle as they stood silently facing her.

'Not a bad evening'.

'No, thank God', Katie replied.

Feeling deflated, Robert sat down on a dry stonewall, attempting to process what he had just heard.

'You mustn't have been expecting that answer', Katie ventured.

'No, I wasn't', he answered honestly.

'I thought that maybe you'd see that I had a point too and that we could come to some compromise, like trying out London for just six or seven months. I didn't think you would slap down my proposal altogether'.

'It would not have worked, Robert. You probably would get used to big money over there, and it would be tempting to stay put.'

'No, I would come back. I would send the money back to you every week, and I would sign a guarantee to that effect in my own blood if you wanted'.

'Like your crowd did when they signed the Solemn Covenant?' she replied, immediately sorry for what she already regarded as a cheap shot.

'Katie, I didn't think you would be one of those jeering me'.

'I am sorry. That was bad form on my part and no hurt intended', she added by way of apology.

'So, what are you saying to me, Katie?'

Are you telling me that the engagement is off or what is it?' he asked, seeking some direction.

She wanted to be one hundred per cent honest with him.

'Robert O' Connor, I love you with all my heart, and I still want to marry you, but I will not wait for you if you go to England. I am afraid it has to be a case of stay with me now or leave me for good'.

Robert's mouth hung open as he attempted to process all of this.

'Then, the decision is made, he added, fighting against his tears as he spoke.

'I would have liked us to be comfortably married with a few pounds in the bank, but if you don't want that, then that's a different story'.

'So, Robert, what exactly are you telling me? Katie needed to know.

This issue had taken up more than enough of her thoughts.

It was now time for clarity and certainty.

She posed a straight question for him to answer.

'Are you staying with me, or are you running from me?'

The coldness and the tone she used in asking that question almost frightened her. As she waited for an answer, her heart skipped a beat.

'Katie, I love you, and because of that love, I will write to Billy Parkes, thank him for his work offer, but tell him that I won't be taking him up on it this time'.

Katie was greatly relieved but was a bit concerned about Robert's attitude.

'What do you mean, this time. How many more times are there going to be?'

'What if Paddy comes back to the yard? I will have no income at all. How can we start married life like paupers?'

'Robert, let's look on the bright side. Right now, both of us are in employment. We love each other and plan to get married. Let's appreciate all that, rather than gloomily looking forward to when we might not be as well set up'.

Robert smiled, recognising that he had failed to win over Katie with his argument.

There was little point in fighting with her.

'I suppose you are right. Come here. I could do with a big hug. You know that you are the best thing to happen to me, don't you?'

'Where would you get better?' she joked as she held out her arms to him.

The embrace following the clearing of the air was warm and tender. After a moment or two, both simultaneously gave a nervous laugh.

'So, we better get working on this wedding then', Robert proposed.

As the couple strolled back up the lane arm in arm, Katie's mother did not have to be told what had transpired. In truth, she did not know whether to be pleased or disappointed.

Katie was in a happier place after their little chat. They had cleared the air, and the future seemed more attractive. They also decided that Robert should approach his employer regarding the letting of his now unoccupied cottage near the graveyard. If that piece of the jigsaw were in position, they would have at least a roof over their heads after the wedding.

Chapter 18

Edward had shown little urgency in advancing plans for his marital home. This delay had infuriated and frustrated Alice.

It was true that he had got the Mc Goldricks, a father and son team, to look over the barn and consider what alterations may be needed. Edward and Gerry were willing to do the labouring on the job in a bid to reduce expense. The Mc Goldricks had plastered the walls, but the roof had not yet been tackled. The real reason for the lack of progress soon became clear.

Edward could not control his rage when he learned that the relationship between his brother and Katie was back on track.

'You could fall into a dung pit and come up smelling of roses, you selfish bastard. That girl should have kicked your miserable arse. Why didn't you stay where you were and let us get on with our lives?'

The outburst shocked all present.

'What the hell is wrong with him?' Robert asked as his brother stormed out of their kitchen. Norah, his sister, was inclined to follow him, but was advised by her mother to stay put.

'Sit down, Love. Your brother is sickening for something, but I don't know what it is. Anyway, he's expecting Alice to call on the way back from her aunt's house'.

That house was just a mile and a half further down the road. The elderly lady had been expecting family home from England, and there was a rush to get the house cleaned in advance of the visit.

Julia had long suspected that Edward had gone cool on Alice. She liked the Kelly girl, and would have viewed her as ideal daughter-in-law material.

Edward was likely to inherit the homestead and assume the ongoing responsibility of caring for Tommy and her into old age. It was important to Julia to have a daughter-in-law that she could get on with. That was for another day. Right now, however, Julia was too young and too independent to consider permitting another woman into her kitchen.

Robert confided in his parents and sister that he hoped to be moving out soon if Mr Murphy agreed to rent the cottage to him.

His mother had mixed opinions on the matter.

'Surely to God, we're in no rush to be rid of you, but I suppose you have to plan for your future. Katie Higgins is a fine sensible girl. She certainly thinks a lot of you, so I trust you won't let her down'.

After his dramatic exit, Edward had returned unnoticed into the room, but his temper had not cooled.

Robert was once again in the firing line.

'You will let Katie down. You always let people down. That is what you do'.

Robert's efforts at self-control were being sorely tested and being found to be wanting.

'Who asked you to put in your tuppence worth? You have your own girl to concern yourself with. Judging by your mood, she mustn't be giving you what you want, or maybe it's a case of you not giving her what she wants, and she's complaining?'

A distraught Julia, deeply upset by the disharmony and nature of the exchange, called for some peace and order.

'That's no way to carry on in a Christian house.'

Edward suspected that Alice might have ridiculed him to his brother,

The very thought of it enraged him.

'What has Alice been saying then?'

Robert did not wish to make any trouble for Alice or for Katie, who had confided that detail in him.

'Alice never mentioned anything about your relationship. You can read into that what you will'.

The atmosphere in the room was turning more and more ugly by the minute.

Julia felt this most of all, and while fighting back the tears, she was vainly pleading with her two sons to calm down and stop the shouting.

'Lord God, will ye quieten down. You are fighting like eight-year-olds when ye should be getting into a state of grace for Mass tomorrow'.

Edward's anger would not be assuaged.

'Are you saying that I can't keep my woman happy?' he charged.

'I am a better man than you will ever be. I stayed and worked this place while you ran away, abandoning Katie Higgins. I will tell you this for nothing. I could have kept Katie happy too if you had not come back. I loved that girl and still do. I am certain that if you had stayed where you were, Katie and I would be together as God intended us to be'.

The bombshell had been dropped and the blast waves had impacted all around it with several moments of stunned silence.

The truth was finally out

Norah was the first to speak.

'Jesus, Mary and Joseph', she blurted out while making the sign of the cross.

'Edward is sickening for Robert's girl. Oh my God!'

Julia watched helplessly as her two sons verbally assaulted one another.

Robert found Edward's sentiments to be both revolting and indicative of a delusional mind.

'So you fancy Katie, do you? You sad bastard', Robert roared at him. 'Katie wouldn't even look at the side of the road you might be on. She prefers a real man, not a dimwit, who spends his time lusting after another man's girl'.

Edward was not to be browbeaten. He again waved an accusing finger at his younger brother.

'I looked out for Katie when you were away with your loyalist friends, and we got very close if you must know. And I know that if you had gone to London, I could be in there', he declared.

There was enough here for Robert to think about, and for a moment, he fell silent.

Edward's sense of triumph was short-lived.

While in full flow, he noticed that his mother's and sister's eyes had suddenly shifted from him onto someone or something behind him. It was much too late when he realised that his girlfriend Alice had overheard the critical part of the exchange. When the loud voices had drowned out her gentle knocking, she had walked unannounced towards the kitchen.

A surreal moment followed as all fell silent and appeared to be frozen in time.

Alice was the first to speak, and she did so in a quivering tone laden with emotion.

'You could have been in there, could you, Edward?'

Let me tell you that I will not marry a man who sees me as nothing more than second best when his preferred choice does not work out'.

Edward was dumbfounded. He could see his future slipping away from him. Rage, combined with sibling animosity, had got the better of him.

'I am sorry, Alice. I was mad with Robert. He provoked me. I didn't mean what I said'.

Alice was not so easily convinced.

'Edward, don't take me for a fool. It all makes perfect sense now. You were just waiting to see how things worked out between Katie and Robert. If they had broken up, and Katie was free, you would have dropped me like a hot potato'.

Edward attempted to embrace her but was rebuffed.

'Don't you dare come near me. I am finished with you. I don't want to see you. I don't want to hear from you, and I sure as hell don't want to marry you. You and Robert can fight to the death over Katie Higgins for all I care. I only hope she's worth it'.

Alice departed in an enraged huff, leaving Edward to his thoughts as he helplessly gazed after her. Julia looked like a mother hen whose clutch had been attacked by a previously harmless vixen. The prospect of a melancholic Edward moping around the house over the summer months was not appealing.

Tommy was bitterly disappointed by the behaviour of his heir apparent.

'Christ almighty, Edward, didn't you know well that the girl intended to call on us? How on earth could you have let her hear the likes of that?'

Edward looked as if his heart could burst at any moment.

'I forgot about her because that bastard maddened me,' he fumed, pointing venomously across the kitchen at his brother Robert.

Julia took a deep breath before flopping down dejectedly in her fireside chair.

It took her several moments to marshal her thoughts.

'Edward, if you were not keen on marrying the girl, you should have said so earlier. I am sure Katie wants no one but Robert. In any case, you should not have been leading Alice a merry dance'.

'I was making a fool of no one, but I was being taken for a fool', Edward roared.

Robert had calmed sufficiently to realise that there could be no winners in a family dispute. He had no wish to see Edward and Alice break up. He could understand that other men might harbour hopes of tempting Katie from him, but he never reckoned that his brother might be one of those. Maybe he had been foolish.

After a period of embarrassing silence, Edward retreated to his bedroom. Norah also retired early, hoping to give the others the space to sift through and possibly salvage something from the ruins of the evening.

Robert and his parents spoke at length but to no avail.

Events had taken a most serious turn.

He was unsure how things might work out, but he knew one thing for sure.

He and Edward could no longer live in the same house.

His parents were entitled to a quiet, peaceful home.

There was nothing more to be said.

Robert had to move out.

Chapter 19

As Mr Murphy was away for the day, Robert's enquiry regarding the availability of the cottage would have to wait. Surprisingly, Alice Kelly reported for work, and acted as if nothing had happened. She may have been suffering from a broken heart, but she performed her duties as before, and with the same pleasant nature. Only that Robert was aware of what happened on Saturday night, he would never have guessed from her demeanour.

During the day, he had little opportunity to engage her in conversation, but he made a point of waiting behind for her when the shop closed in the evening. She seemed slightly uncomfortable when she saw him, but that was not surprising.

'I'll walk a bit with you,' he said in a matter-of-fact tone.

Alice did not have a problem with that.

'So, tell me, Alice, is it all over with Edward or can things be patched up?' he asked.

Alice sighed.

'It's definitely over, and it has been over for a long time, only that your brother didn't think it worthwhile to tell me. I had to overhear it on Saturday night'.

'When he sees sense, he'll want to put things right with you'.

Alice shook her head forlornly.

'Patch it up…put things right; I don't want a patched-up relationship. I don't want to be the second choice of any man'.

Robert had no intention of pushing Edward's case despite feeling guilty about their break-up. Had he been less aggressive, Alice and Edward might be in a different situation now. Whether that would be for the better or not, nobody could say. Alice told him Edward had called around to her house on Sunday to apologise for his behaviour.

Interestingly, he did not express a desire to get back with her.

'Your brother just called to put a more pleasant ending to the relationship, like he was tying up the loose strings. He said he was sorry that I had overheard him, but he did not apologise for what he said. Of course, he blamed you for provoking him, but from what I can make out, he was relieved that it brought things to a head with us'.

Her voice began to quiver with this acknowledgment.

Alice had to accept that her relationship with Edward had irretrievably broken down. She harboured no residual bitterness, but her self-worth had taken a body blow. Nevertheless, the girl was made of stern stuff, and she would rise again. However, she feared that she could never implicitly trust a man again.

'Alice, it might look bad now, but I don't think you should bury the relationship until you are certain it is dead'.

'It is definitely over between Edward and me. I will have to look elsewhere for a husband. I'll stand by the wall at the dances again. I will have to compete with the younger girls, but I will get another fellow, and I will make sure no man will mess me around again', she vowed.

Robert felt guilty that his brother had caused her so much heartache. Instinctively, he threw his arms around her and held her tight.

'I'm sorry you were messed around, and if it is over with Edward, I hope you find another who will treat you like the lady you are'.

Alice brightened on hearing these tender and complimentary words from such an unexpected source.

'Thank you, I appreciate your kind words'.

For the first time, the cracks in Alice's tough facade began to appear.

'What is it about me anyway, Robert?

Why am I no match for Katie Higgins with either O'Connor man?'

That question was highly revealing and difficult for Robert to answer.

He shifted uncomfortably on his feet as he attempted to frame a response.

'It's not a reflection on you at all and in a way it is a case of the forbidden fruit being sweeter. Isn't that what people say? For Edward, Katie was the forbidden fruit"

'And who is the forbidden fruit for you, Robert?

The younger O' Connor looked embarrassed.

Is there a girl somewhere that you are lusting after, or is Katie woman enough for you both?'

Robert chose not to answer.

'I never asked you this before, but what does Katie make of Edward's feelings for her?'

Robert had not got a chance to discuss it with Katie yet.

'She doesn't know yet, but I'm sure she'll be surprised'.

'I hope she doesn't think the second brother could do the same thing'.

'Ah no, Katie trusts me. She knows that I am not like Edward'.

'That's true. You are a bit taller and more full of yourself', she wryly responded.

Alice again asked how Katie might react to Edward carrying a torch for her.

'I suppose she'd be embarrassed and want to keep out of his way'.

Alice claimed that she would not feel embarrassed if the positions had been reversed.

'I'd be flattered if I were in her position'.

'You would not.'

'I most certainly would. I think that it would be dead romantic, but maybe not coming from a bloke like Edward'.

Robert was growing increasingly uncomfortable with this line of conversation and quickly brought it to an end. Later that night, he replayed the conversation in his mind and considered what she had said. It was all very interesting and highly revealing.

Chapter 20

On Tuesday, Robert was delighted to discover that his employer was more than willing to rent him the isolated cottage.

'You'd be doing me a huge favour. That place is better occupied, and a man like you, that's handy, might keep it in shape'.

With such a positive reception, Robert wondered why he had been worried about the request at all.

'There are very few people willing to rent that place, Robert. The graveyard puts most of them off. I had the prospect of a tenant there some months ago, but it never came to anything. One look at the place was enough to put him off'.

'I will rent the cottage to you for the nominal fee of one penny a week, providing you agree to carry out the running repairs. You can pick up whatever you need in the yard, be that nails, glass, or paint. I have the lease agreement somewhere and I will root that out for you to sign'.

Robert understood that the payment of a nominal rent was to avoid the unlikely risk of his gaining squatter's rights to the property. Murphy was a decent sort, and he was entitled to protect his assets. Robert readily agreed to carry out whatever running repairs might be needed.

Katie was delighted at the news about the cottage. However, she ruled out the earlier suggestion of a double wedding for the O' Connor clan. She wanted to have her own day out, so when his sister's wedding was out of the way, Robert and she would finalise arrangements for their big day.

October was provisionally pencilled in as the likely time.

Later that evening, Robert and Katie went to view the cottage. They had passed by the house on dozens of occasions, but neither of them had stepped inside yet.

The cottage was like something out of a fairytale or even a horror story. It displayed all the signs of abandonment, with cracked windows, peeling paint and gutters clogged with debris from the overhanging trees. The graveyard was practically on its doorstep. One could easily have kicked a football from the front door right onto one of the graves.

On opening the front door, they were met by the distinctive musty smell of an unoccupied house. The place badly needed an airing. Katie rushed to open the front windows, and Robert left the door open to allow in as much fresh air as possible. The prospective tenant that Alice mentioned took one look at it and decided that it was not for him. Both could understand his reaction.

The old fashioned kitchen was very small and cramped, with an open fireplace dominating the space. Two doors on either side of the kitchen led to the two bedrooms.

There was certainly a backlog of dusting and cleaning to be done, but a day or two could see huge progress. Some randomly placed sticks in the fireplace helped draw Robert's attention to the chimney. Just as he thought, birds had been attempting to build a nest in the chimney and had probably succeeded.

'I'll have to get a chimney brush up there. Katie. There is probably an old nest up there from a few years back'.

They looked through the bedrooms. The bases and mattresses seemed good, but they would need to buy sheets and pillowcases.

The small cottage windows, together with the overhanging branches denied all but the bare minimum of light to the bedrooms. They would well need to have a light on for most of the year in those rooms if he didn't cut some of the branches.

Katie did not want her man to catch cold or pneumonia on a damp mattress.

'You should carry them outside on the first good day'.

Robert and Katie knew that the accommodation was far from perfect, but they were confident they could transform it into a cosy, little home. Before departure, Robert made a mental list of what was needed to make it habitable.

Most of those items could be picked up from his workplace.

'You should change the lock on the door, Katie suggested.

'You don't want unexpected visitors, now, do you?'

'Not unless they are good looking', he said.

Katie feigned a smile, but was not amused.

After a moment or two, spent luxuriating in the thought of having their own space, Robert eventually updated her on the Edward and Alice drama.

Katie listened in horror. She was disappointed that Edward and Alice had broken up.

'You know, Alice kept my spirits up when you were away. She was always up for a laugh, and Edward was like a big brother to me, always checking to see if I wanted anything or needed to go anywhere. Between the two of them, they kept me sane', she said.

'Well, Edward wasn't acting out of selflessness, was he? He wasn't interested in any of that big brother nonsense.'

'What do you mean?'

'Well, it all came out on Saturday night. Edward and I had a blazing row and both of us said things we should not have said. Anyway, the upshot was he claimed he would be a better husband for you than I ever could. He even went to far as to confess that he loved you'.

Despite her initial doubt about Robert winding her up, Katie soon realised that he was deadly serious.

'God Almighty!' Katie said.

She could not think of anything she had ever said or done to make Edward think that she could have a romantic interest in him.

She was astonished to hear that Alice had walked in on this and overheard some very hurtful things.

'Poor Alice, I'm sure she wished that the ground could have opened and swallowed her up. Imagine your world being shattered in such a cruel and public way by someone you had given your heart to'.

Katie was keen to know the lead up to the shouting match between the brothers.

Robert did his best to report the incident as faithfully as possible while she hung on every word.

'That was so awful. It's a terrible pity that neither Edward nor you could control your temper'.

Robert attempted to defend himself in this regard, but Katie was having none of it.

'Ye are grown men, yet ye were fighting like schoolboys, with each trying to get the better of the other. But I pity Alice most. She suffered most in this'.

Robert explained that she seemed to be coping pretty well with the devastating blow.

'I talked to her this evening. She is gutted, I know, but she feels that Edward did her a favour in one way. He was stalling things with her until he saw how things worked out with us'.

'I feel for the poor girl, but I don't accept that she could be coping as well as you say she is. The poor girl is just putting on a brave face and getting on with life, but don't imagine that any girl could just sail through something like this'.

Edward was now becoming a major problem for Katie. She dreaded their next meeting. She asked Robert how his brother was coping with the latest turn of events.

'Edward is moping about a bit. He went to Alice's house on Sunday to apologise for her hearing it that way, but there was no mention of wanting to patch things up with her'.

Katie squirmed in disgust.

'How can I ever look him in the face again? I never gave him the slightest indication that I was interested in him'.

'You didn't have to. It was all wishful thinking on his part, although I can't blame any man for fancying you'.

Katie did not consider that it was a time for levity on anyone's part. 'This is no laughing matter, Robert. I remember Edward being so kind to me. He would rescue me whenever the likes of Pat Mc Manus got awkward, and he would dance me around the dance floor while he left Alice sitting there. Maybe, I am stupid that did not suspect anything earlier'.

'But, how could you possibly know? How could you tell that his concern was anything more than looking out for his brother's girl?' Anyway, you never told me Pat Mc Manus was hassling you. That bloke sounds as if he needs a few slaps'.

This was not what Katie wanted to hear.

'You listen to me. Pat Mc Manus is a creep, but he never laid a finger on me. And you, you with all your talk of slapping people. Has the war taught you anything at all?'

'OK, don't get yourself worked up about it. I was only saying'.

'That's fine, then, but do you think I have lost Alice as a friend? Robert assured her that although Alice was hurting now she was already showing signs of recovering.

'Listen, Katie, don't you forget that you are the innocent party here. You just happened to be more attractive to Edward than Alice was. You did not plan it. You did not even know it. You are not to blame'.

Chapter 21

Katie sought to avoid meeting Edward face to face, but she bumped right into him outside the post office.

They both seemed equally shocked and uncomfortable at the encounter. An embarrassing silence ensued, as they stood there, anxious, no doubt, that this casual encounter might put an end to any awkwardness between them.

It was Edward who first managed to string a few words together.

'I know that I made a fool out of myself and embarrassed you. I want to tell you that I'm sorry for causing you any hurt'.

Katie acknowledged the apology, but suggested that Alice is the one he should be apologising to'.

Edward assured her that he had already done so.

'I called over to her house and told her that I was sorry', he replied sheepishly, his eyes directed downwards.

'Edward, you must know that I never encouraged you into thinking that there was anything romantic between us. Robert was always the only man for me'.

He acknowledged what he was hearing, but sought to explain his take on events.

'I understood that, but I always had this feeling that if he wasn't on the scene, then maybe you might have...'

Katie was keen to scotch that notion once and for all.

'Edward, that was never going to happen. You were with Alice, and you were well suited. You must know that even if there were no Robert, we could never be in a romantic relationship'.

That rather brutal statement stung Edward. He raised his eyes as his embarrassed look quickly gave way to a more assertive and contrary one.

'My younger brother is not the great man you might think he is. He picked you up, played with you, and then when the novelty wore off, he headed to the war in search of more excitement. He was only back a couple of months, and he was ready for off again. I would never treat you like that, Katie'.

Katie was now beginning to feel distinctly uncomfortable. Even the way he uttered her name had sent a shiver down her spine.

It was clear to her the man was delusional.

He held some crazy, possessive feelings towards her, and even her talking to him was enough to give oxygen to those feelings.

That situation had to end.

Tough words had to be said, and now was the time to say them, lest he might pursue her to the pearly gates in the belief that there might still be hope for him.

She steeled herself to be measured and unequivocal.

'Edward, get this into your head once and for all. I am with Robert. I will stay with Robert, and even if Robert were to vanish from this planet in the morning, I would never be your girlfriend. That is no personal reflection on you. That is true for the entire male population of the county', she added, stretching out both arms to emphasise the scope of the area.

'I think more of you than Robert does', he said in a childlike sulky tone.

The man was not for listening.

'Even if you loved me ten times as much as you say you do, it would make no difference Edward because I don't love you. Even if it is off with Alice, there are plenty of other women around who would be flattered with your attention, but I am not one of them'.

She allowed that point to register before she spoke again.

'Now, has that point got through to you?'

Edward acknowledged that he had heard, but it was not sinking in.

'You will regret this, Katie'.

'Well, I will have to take that chance'.

'You are still the girl for me. We will be together when you get over all the nonsense and see the light'.

There was little point in taking up any more of her time.

Katie realised that Edward was determined to believe his preferred reality.

'You are deluding yourself, Edward, and I will not feed into that. I am walking away from here now, and the next time I meet you, I will not listen to immature drivelling or help me God, I'll knock that senseless head clean off your shoulders'.

Katie walked away and left him standing there, still claiming that she would soon see the light. As she turned the corner, she allowed herself a sigh of relief at the top of the village. She needed to rest for a moment. Her legs had become weak and her hands were shaking, but she had remained strong when she needed to'.

She was upset by what had just transpired, but she was also proud of her composure and courage. She did not have to think up what she was saying.

The words just flowed naturally. Edward may not want to hear what she had said, but surely the realisation that he was wasting his time would soon set in for him. At least, that was the hope.

Chapter 22

Robert might only have been at home for two months, but his mother, Julia, still felt sad when he moved out. She was still hurting because of the bad blood between her sons, but she did not hold her younger son responsible for it all.

Robert was on the path to marrying a good woman, and who could blame poor Edward? The man loved and lost. She hoped that he would re-emerge to take on the world once he had recovered from his emotional trauma.

Julia was glad that Robert would still be nearby. She would still be able to see him whenever she wished. As he was departing, she made Robert promise to visit them every week despite the bad blood between the brothers.

Julia was being surprisingly upbeat.

'Don't you worry. Edward is a good boy. He will do what his mammy tells him. Pretty soon, all this fuss will be forgotten. Then, we can get on like a normal family again'.

Ever since the showdown, the two brothers were seldom, if ever, together for breakfast, dinner, supper or the family rosary. Robert had not changed his schedule, but Edward always managed to be out of the house whenever Robert called.

'Where is he now, Ma?'

'He's gone up to Mick Kelly to ask him to mow the big meadow for us. The weather is supposed to pick up after tomorrow'.

Tommy was bored and exasperated by the drama surrounding Edward and Robert. He coped as he often did by being facetious. This helped to release tension for him

'Surely one woman is much the same as the next, and what would be wrong if Edward took Katie and you swapped her for Alice. Wouldn't you all be happy then?'

Julia was having none of that sort of talk.

'Listen here, Tommy, I know you are messing, but anyone listening to you may not know that, and you appear a total fool altogether'.

Tommy laughed and wondered where all these eavesdroppers might be hiding.

'Sure, there's only ourselves here'.

'I pity Alice', Robert said.

'She is the big loser in all of this'.

His father begged to differ.

'I don't see it that way. Wasn't the girl was lucky to learn the truth before it was too late to do anything about it? Alice is one fine girl and will get a new man. I'd have chanced my luck with her if I were thirty years younger'.

Julia was none too impressed with her husband's pronouncements on Alice.

'Chance your luck with her. At your age, you should be down on your knees with your rosary beads, praying for a happy death and not looking at youngsters like Alice Kelly'.

Tommy took the predictable admonishing with typical good grace.

'I'm only making a point, Love. You know that I have only eyes for you'

Robert deliberately left a few possessions behind for his mother's sake to keep alive the illusion that this was nothing more than a temporary departure. Robert always intended to be a regular visitor. His mother played along, as did his father, who resumed his fireside seat as he might for some routine departure.

Julia walked her son to the door and seemingly casually patted him on the shoulder as he left. After all, he was only going up the road. He was not leaving the country.

Chapter 23

Every five or six years, a team of dedicated preachers from one of the specialist orders would arrive in a parish in a campaign of spiritual renewal. This was known simply as The Mission. For those who had become a little lax about their faith, this was intended to get back on the path to eternal salvation. The methods of the Mission priests might vary from order to order, but it was frequently a case of the hard cop/soft cop double-act.

The parish priest, Fr Maguire, had booked two priests from the Redemptorist Order. These men were reputed to be inspirational speakers with impressive academic credentials. The accolade of 'great preacher' was one of the highest compliments paid to such a cleric. One could rightly expect rhetorical brilliance and captivating theatrics. The congregation at the various talks, which often included members of other religious denominations, wanted a performance. The Mission could be seen as a religious version of a carnival and was eagerly anticipated by all.

Religious hawkers, who had been awarded the exclusive franchise, sold their wares in the church grounds. The area around the church was like a mini Knock with rosary beads, scapulars, statues and other assorted religious paraphernalia. All items purchased would be blessed during the week.

The senior cleric leading the Mission was Rev Mark Howard, a man with thirty years of service in the order. His assistant was a young man in his late thirties who wished to be known as Fr Mike. It was already clear to the congregation who the 'hard cop' would be on this occasion.

These hard men, like the villains in the movies, were the crowd pullers. They could call down fire and brimstone, and scare the living daylights out of everyone in the congregation and they would gladly return the following night for more.

On Sunday, June 16, the Mission opened. The Mission priests had already been introduced at the morning Masses. Fr Howard outlined the programme of events and a timetable for talks, confessions and visitations.

On opening night, there was a great sense of anticipation especially in relation to Wednesday and Thursday nights. These nights focused on sins of the flesh. Discussion of sexual matters was enough to guarantee a packed house and raise temperatures in the congregations. The parishioners was segregated on these nights. This all added to the feeling that this would be heavy-duty stuff. Women's night was scheduled for Wednesday and men's night for Thursday. Other nights covered such important but more boring topics as Penance, Renewal and Bearing Witness.

On opening night, the church was packed to capacity and beyond. Fr. Mark Howard gave the religious equivalent of a keynote address. He made sure to insert the name of the parish and the village regularly in his talk. This helped give the congregation a feeling of importance and inclusion. He spoke of the changing times, the threats to traditional practice and the increasing trend of secularisation that was evident in the post-war world.

'Your forefathers suffered terribly in past centuries. They were denied the right to openly practise their religion. They were forced to assemble and pray at Mass rocks and holy wells during the dreaded Penal Laws. They died in the hundreds during the Great Famine. Cruel landlords evicted many of them from their holdings, but during all that trouble and all that pain, they remained steadfastly loyal to the Mass, to the Holy Rosary and the commandments of God.

Today, however, there is a new generation of people in this parish. Life has been somewhat kinder to them. This generation has seen greater security of tenure, national self-determination and greater economic prospects, but is this generation losing out on something? Is this generation as pleasing to God? Is this generation gone soft on religious observance?

If you wish to avoid eternal suffering in the flames of Hell, you should turn your backs on the temptations of this world and instead focus on securing a place at the right hand of God. Then, in the presence of our glorious ancestors, we will praise God forever and ever.

Each evening before the talk, Fr. Mike and I will hear Confessions We will act as a medium between you and God. Penance and prayer are gifts from God to us, and they are given to us so that we may find that way back to God'.

Chapter 24

Robert arrived in the church just as the leader of the Mission led the congregation through an examination of their consciences. He systematically went through all the commandments, but laid a particular emphasis on the sixth commandment.

'Did I harbour impure thoughts?'

'Did I covet my neighbour's wife or girlfriend, and was I a source of scandal to others in this regard?'

Robert wondered what Edward might make of this.

It was a long time since Robert had attended Confession, but the urgings of his mother and fiancée proved too strong to resist. As Confessions started, he sought to join the queue for the young priest, but his line was much too long for a man in a hurry.

He even considered doing a runner, but thought better of it. After all, everyone was lining up for Confession. There was nothing for it but to brave the formidable Fr Mark Howard. The priest seemed surprised that Robert had not seen the inside of a confessional for nearly three years.

He was even more surprised to discover that he had joined the British Army and fought in the war, and the man was utterly astounded to learn that this penitent had chosen to enlist in a Northern Protestant regiment.

'Young man, in your relatively short life, you seem to have a penchant for making wrong choices. What prevailed upon you to ally yourself with such men?'

Robert had no intention of apologising for anything he had done. Rather, he seemed to enjoy upsetting the older priest.

'Well, Father, de Valera was keen to keep us out of the war, and I can understand his reasons. I saw Catholic countries like France and Belgium being overrun by the Nazis, and I felt I had to do my bit to help them'.

Robert might have impressed one of the local men with such logic, but the mission priest was far from impressed.

'So, to defend Catholic countries, you joined a force with one of the most anti-Catholic outfits in Europe. Even Adolf Hitler himself was likely to have been more pro-Catholic. To the best of my recollections, he may even have been baptized a Catholic'.

'He may have been Father, but didn't he have a sight of priests killed?'

The priest quickly sensed that he was dealing with a man who could not be easily intimidated.

'Perhaps, but tell me again, which Northern regiment did you join?'

'Royal Ulster Rifles, Father'.

'Oh, the very name sounds repulsive. I can't say that I heard very much about them'.

Robert had remembered what Joseph Murphy had read in the newspaper and he relayed this to Fr Howard.

'According to what I have heard, Father, we were the only regiment to be present at Normandy both as an air force and a ground force'.

The priest was unimpressed.

'Listen here, young man. You talk about this as if it was a great thing. Your first duty is not to your country or the King of England either. Your first duty is to save your eternal soul, and you will not do that consorting with the enemy'.

'Father, I swear, we never consorted with the enemy. We were always with other Allied forces'.

'Good heavens, you man of little wit. I refer to dangers to your faith, not to your physical safety. One day, you will leave your earthly body behind you, and return to the dust in your local cemetery, but your soul is eternal. You have a duty to treasure it and keep it pure'.

Robert nodded his agreement through the grille. He was desperately hoping that this man would give him a quick absolution and release him. He already knew that there would be comments about how long he was in the confessional.

'Tell me, young man was any provision made for your spiritual welfare during your time with those men?'

'We had a chaplain, Father'.

'A Protestant minister, I presume. You might as well have Charlie Chaplin for all the use he would be. Did you attend Mass or receive Holy Communion during hostilities?'

'No, not Mass, but I sat in on the different services now and again. You know it's the same God after all.'

Robert realised that he had lobbed a verbal grenade into the conversation. He could distinctly hear a sharp intake of breath from the opposite side of the grille.

He delighted in believing that he was a source of annoyance to the educated priest.

'The same God, you say. Do you, a simple peasant boy from the hills of North Leitrim, presume to trade theology with me? Forget this nonsense about the same God. There is one true God and one true Church that Christ left us with when he was assumed into Heaven'.

'Yes, Father'!'

Robert took great pleasure in unsettling a man he considered arrogant and condescending. He had earlier wondered what his prescribed penance might be. Robert thought he might escape with maybe three Rosaries to recite at the outset. Now, he considered that he might well have to recite one hundred rosaries while walking backwards to Knock Shrine.

Fr Mark was not finished with him yet. He wished to know about Robert's sexual experiences during his time in the army. He asked whether he had touched himself or touched other soldiers. There had not been much of that sort of thing going on in the regiment.

The priest was equally keen to know whether Robert had touched women, either over or under their clothing.

'We saw very few women, Father and those we did see, I was not near enough to touch any of them'.

Robert would have said anything that might have brought a quick end to his inquisition. He would have confessed to adultery even though he was still unmarried.

The priest seemed marginally less than apoplectic with his responses to those questions. He urged him to pray hard for the gift of purity. He should see the body of any girl he might encounter as being a tabernacle of God.

'If you keep that image in your mind, you will not go far wrong'.

Robert was tempted to respond that one would do precious little with such a mental picture, but he did not wish to prolong the engagement for one second more.

Fr. Howard was taken aback to learn that the penitent was already engaged and was informed that he had been in a pre-war relationship that had been put in mothballs for two and a half years.

'The girl you speak of is either a saint or a fool, and I am not able to say which'.

Just as Robert feared that he would start upon a second half-hour in the box, the priest lifted his hand to grant him absolution but not before giving him his penance.

'For your penance, I want you to recite the Holy Rosary three times daily for the rest of the month and offer them up for the Souls in Purgatory'.

The absolution was prescribed. The grille was closed, and Robert emerged red-faced and chastened.

He went with the others to the post Confession space near the back of the church, where one supposedly started on one's penance.

Robert was in no mood to say his penance then and doubted if he would ever say it. He was not repentant for anything that he had done. He considered that he had once again become the whipping boy for others. As far as he was concerned, he would never see the inside of a confession box again.

Chapter 25

June 23 was a Sunday, and ordinarily, no servile work was permitted on the Sabbath. However, the weather had been so wet that the harvest was in danger of being lost. Fr. Maguire announced that working in the hayfields would not be a sin.

Katie was delighted that Robert could join her father and brother in haymaking. Her fiancé was now an accepted part of the Higgins family. She loved Robert's company in the meadows. It was great to watch his strong manly frame stoop to lift huge, weighty pitchforks of sweet-smelling hay before piling them on the haycocks.

In recent weeks, Gerry Higgins had not been feeling the best and was far from being meadow fit. Nevertheless, he busied himself with the less strenuous tasks of shaping and trimming the haycocks and making the hay ropes that would secure the finished product.

Josie Taylor had also been enticed into the hayfield. Josie had a very easy-going attitude to life. He loved to chat and did not exert himself with physical labour.

Robert enjoyed this man's company and was looking forward to a good light-hearted atmosphere there.

'Did you go to Confession for the mission?' Gerry asked Josie.

'I did indeed. I went to that young man. I didn't fancy the look of the older one. He looked sour, and he seemed to be keeping people for a very long time'.

Robert suspected that this was Josie having a bit of harmless fun at his expense, but he refused to rise to the bait.

'What did you think of the mission anyway, Josie?' Robert was keen to know.

'Well, there was a lot less shouting and craw thumping than the last time. The old lad is a great preacher, but I feel the younger man isn't the finished article yet. He is a bit soft on penitents. Few of that outfit will let you off with three Hail Marys during a mission'.

It was thirsty work in the meadows, and Robert felt the need to return to the house for a drink. It was less a case of thirst than needing a break from the hard work. Katie followed him, delighted to have him to herself, if only for a few minutes.

While they were chatting, she enquired about his recent experience with his nightmares.

There had been some improvement in the situation.

'I still find myself waking up in a cold sweat, with the noise of shells and gunfire in my head'.

'That should pass', Katie optimistically said, placing her slender arm on his for reassurance.

'Yea, everything passes, I suppose, even ourselves', Robert answered without real conviction. He was keen to move away from this uncomfortable topic.

Looking with some urgency in the direction of the hayfield, he made a suggestion.

'I think we will have the whole field up by seven, so we'll have time to clean up and go down to the bonfire. There is bound to be a bit of fun at the crossroads'.

As they returned to the hayfield, they were teased mercilessly.

'We know what you two have been up to', Joseph shouted.

Josie asked whether anyone else had heard the sound of creaking bedsprings.

Gerry discouraged anything that was suggestive or smutty but he liked to see young people laugh.

'It must be great to be young and have your whole life in front of you'.

Katie and Robert did not get to the bonfire that night after all. Circumstances soon put paid to that.

Chapter 26

Later in the night, Gerry complained of severe stabbing pain in his chest. He had complained of low-level chest pains for some time and attributed them to indigestion or heartburn. The pain stubbornly refused to go away on this occasion, and the man's face took on a greyer complexion. The family decided to err on the side of caution and send for the doctor.

A new dispensary doctor had arrived in the village, replacing the recently retired Dr Mick. The new doctor was Peter Clarke, a giant of a man with a very cheery disposition. He was alone yet, but a wife and young children would be joining him shortly. The few who had attended him in the dispensary reported that he was a man you could say anything to. This was as good a reference as one could give a doctor. Airs and graces did not go down well in North Leitrim in 1946.

As the doctor was unfamiliar with the area, Joseph was dispatched to act as navigator. There were concerns that the new man might be annoyed at being called out on a Sunday evening, but they did not lightly summon him.

About an hour later, the doctor's car pulled up on the their front street. The small and narrow doorway was soon darkened by the sheer bulk of the new doctor.

A cheery greeting was extended to all present, and immediately fears of an angry medic dissipated. The man was possessed of a loud, booming voice that might easily be heard in the furthest house in the townland. Margaret Higgins ushered the doctor into her husband's bedroom, where he was still lying above the bedclothes.

'How are you, my good man? I hear you are not feeling the best.'

The sick man muttered something incomprehensible.

'I see. You look a little wishy-washy.

Where does it hurt?'

Gerry's right hand traced from the left-hand side of his chest down along his left arm.

'I see, in the chest and a bit down the arm. If you don't mind, I will listen to your chest'.

Even though it was warm in the house, the doctor blew on the stethoscope to warm it. He placed it on the sick man's chest and listened. His expression remained inscrutable throughout the examination.

He asked Margaret some questions about her husband's recent condition. She told him about the occasional bouts of what he presumed to be indigestion or heartburn. Dr Clarke nodded throughout and kept saying 'I know… I know… I know' as he viewed the readings of the blood pressure gauge.

All the indicators pointed in one direction, but not wishing to alarm the patient, Dr Clarke maintained his casual tone.

'It's better to take no chances. It might well be nothing, but I want to have a few tests done on you, Gerry. I'm sending you to Manorhamilton Hospital for a few days. There is nothing to worry your head about at all.'

'Is my heart about to give up?' Gerry asked, wincing with pain as he spoke.

'Your heart will last you as long as you are in it'.

It was a statement of the obvious, but it seemed to reassure Gerry.

Margaret was all a flutter, wondering how quickly she could organise things for Gerry.

'I have his clean pyjamas ready, but Katie, will you get his razor and soap, and if you get a pair of his Long Johns from the bottom drawer in our room'.

Dr Clarke was anxious to calm things down a little lest Gerry's blood pressure be adversely impacted.

'Were you ever in the hospital before, Gerry?

'I was never in the hospital. I got my tonsils out when I was younger, but that was in the dispensary in the village'.

'Yea and I suppose you had to walk home afterwards?' questioned the doctor.

That had been the case.

'My father had the same story. Men were made tough then'.

Although feeling the pain, Gerry was still able to offer a faint smile.

The doctor was doing his best to ease the understandable fears of the patient.

'Well, Our Lady's is a lovely little hospital, and I know the matron there. She's a lovely lady and you are a lovely man, so you are in luck', he joked.

'My brother from America is in the country, Doctor; I hope I am still around to see him when he gets up to these parts.'

'And why wouldn't you? Unless you are planning to skip the country.'

The doctor returned to the kitchen, where Katie had a basin of warm water and a towel waiting for him to wash his hands.

'What do you think, Doctor?' she asked directly.

'Well, it's hard to tell very much, but I think it's a bit more serious than heartburn. His blood pressure is up, and he seems to have tightness in the chest area. Worryingly, he talks of pains down his arm. I think he might have suffered a slight heart attack, so I'd like him to go to the hospital to be on the safe side'.

Katie was worried. The doctor was quite up-front with her, and the truth alarmed her.

Margaret arrived in the kitchen excitedly, throwing folded laundry into a small cardboard suitcase as she moved from press to press.

'Now calm down, Mrs Higgins', the doctor pleaded.

'Sure, I don't want to be coming back to treat you tomorrow'.

'Do you think he'll get over this, doctor?' she asked, with eyes desperate for reassurance.

'He'll be in the very best hands, and sure with any luck at all, he'll be back before you even notice he's gone'.

Chapter 27

Doctor Clarke drove Gerry to the hospital. Margaret sat in the back with her husband, and wrapped him warmly in the tartan rug provided. Katie sat in the front passenger seat, giving the occasional backward glance, attempting to assess both her father's condition and her mother's stress levels. True to form, Dr Clarke kept the mood positive.

'A couple of days rest will do a lot for Gerry. With all the wet weather, it's been a tough time for the farmers. Sure, it's a constant worry about getting the hay saved at all'.

'Are you from farming stock?' Margaret wanted to know.

'Well, my grandfather was a small farmer, and I spent a lot of my summers working on the small farm he had. My father had a drapery shop in County Roscommon, where I grew up'.

The patient in the back was feeling a little better, at least good enough to ask about the size of the grandfather's farm.

It was less than thirty acres of poor enough land outside Ballaghaderreen, on the Gurteen Road. I remember when people used to ask how big the farm was, my grandfather used to say that he had the 'place of four cows and a bicycle'.

'There's not much living to be made on the land now, Doctor', Gerry whispered.

'Never was Gerry, never was unless you had some of the quality land, like what they have up there in Kildare and Meath.'

'They are a different class of farmer altogether', Margaret conceded.

'So, you are having Yanks' the doctor probed. 'Will the brother be staying with you?'

'He will, Doctor, God help me, and his wife and a big lug of a son! I don't know how I'll manage'.

'Well, I am sure they will be spoiled rotten'.

The doctor joked that they probably wouldn't want to go back to America at all.

Katie was growing a little less concerned as they came towards the end of the eight-mile trip to the hospital. Her father was at least stable, but she was too stressed to engage in small talk. She politely answered the doctor's questions about what she was up to, and she took great pleasure in telling him that she would soon be a blushing bride.

'Isn't that great altogether. Love is what makes the world go around.'

'Will you both go with Gerry into *Admissions*, and I will drop into the Matron's Office and see if she's there. I have to give her some background on the patient and his symptoms'.

His wife and daughter assisted Gerry into the hospital. The place smelled very strongly of cleaning agents and disinfectants. Margaret and Katie used the cubicle provided to help Gerry change into his pyjamas.

Some moments later, the doctor returned in the company of a smiling, fresh-faced nun wearing a white veil.

'Ah Matron, this is Gerry. He's been having pains in his chest, and we don't want to take any chances.'

The Matron exchanged quick handshakes with Gerry and the two women.

Her comments were directed towards the sick man.

'Now, Gerry, what we are going to do is have the house doctor give you a quick look over. After that, we will get you to bed for a good rest. And I hope you will be feeling much better in the morning'.

There was no more to be said. The Matron escorted Gerry to his bed, and the others went home.

Chapter 28

Gerry had suffered a slight heart attack, and he was to be monitored in hospital for ten days. However, it was clear that Gerry's days of doing hard physical work were over. Joseph would have to assume more responsibility on the farm. The young lad did not mind this in the slightest. He was grateful that his father would be returning home. Robert felt that he was obliged to volunteer his assistance whenever he could, but with a job to hold down, he could not be relied upon to be there when needed.

Katie worried about her father, and this robbed her of her usual good cheer. That was not her only worry.

She was also a bit worried about Robert. Although he constantly denied it, she had the lingering impression that he somehow resented her blocking his move to London. He had said nothing, but something like feminine intuition informed her that he saw himself forever trapped as a wage slave in a dead-end job. She suspected that he blamed her for missing out on his one chance of obtaining financial security. Still, they seemed to be getting on pretty well, and the wedding was tentatively pencilled in for early October.

Katie's relationship with Alice had changed for the worse. The warmth that had flowed between them in previous times had disappeared. Katie was saddened by this but wasn't at all surprised. She had tried to imagine how she might have felt if the situation had been reversed. It must have been a mortifying experience. She wondered how the girl could summon the strength to drag herself out of bed every day, much less put on a cheery face for the world to see.

Katie had already spoken to Robert about this, but he could not understand her concerns. As far as he could see, Alice was coping pretty well. They spoke regularly at work, and she seemed to be getting on with her life. He had felt that because it was his brother who had let her down, he might well be a target for her anger. That had not happened, and he believed that he had a very courteous and friendly relationship with the girl.

Alice happened to walk through Murphy's yard on Tuesday, just as Katie had been bringing Robert up to date on Gerry's condition. She made a point of approaching her to politely enquire about her father's condition.

'Katie, what's the latest on your father?'

Katie was grateful for the polite enquiry and hoped it marked a return to more normal interaction between them.

'They say he's stable, so I suppose that's as much as we can hope for'.

'Well, tell him I was asking for him and that we are all thinking of him and saying the odd prayer'.

'Well, I will indeed, Alice and thank you for asking'.

Alice headed back into Murphy's kitchen, and Katie continued her chat with Robert. The pair arranged to meet later and spend some time making the cottage more habitable. Before meeting up with Katie, Robert decided to visit his family. His mother and his sister, Norah, had been to Sligo, and had just returned as he cycled up to the homestead. Norah's wedding was just over a month away, and she had been getting her trousseau organised.

Hughie was due over later in the evening, but of course, he was barred from getting even a glimpse of the outfit, not that Hughie was particularly bothered anyway.

'What's it like anyway? Robert asked.

'Well, it's a white flowing dress, high- waist with a bell-shaped bottom….'

'Well, that's lost on me. You can tell Katie when you see her. She will know what you are talking about'.

'You might have to write that down for me'.

Norah smiled, recognising the potential truth of this.

'Has Katie got her bride's outfit yet?' Norah enquired.

Robert shook his head.

'No, I think we'll see you and Hughie off first',

Robert felt that the house would be very strange when his sister moved out.

Since she could stand up in the kitchen, Norah seemed to be helping her mother bake scones and tarts and prepare the dinners for the family. She had been her mother's faithful assistant for years now. He knew that his mother would miss her.

Julia realised this all too well, but she was pleased that her daughter was getting married and especially pleased that she was getting into such a good holding. Hughie would look after her well, of that she had no doubt. They had grown very close together.

Norah had never been one for the spotlight. Like other young girls, she had enjoyed the dance hall for socialising. The family occupied all her interests and efforts. She always seemed to be more mature than her peer group. If marriages were initiated only from dancehall encounters and beauty contests, Norah and Hughie might never have walked down the aisle. However, thanks to the help of family and friends, the match was made, and a good one at that.

Edward wandered in before Robert left for the village. The brothers grunted an acknowledgement of each other's presence, which was as good as it was likely to get between them. Tommy was interested to hear how to work on the cottage was proceeding. Robert updated him, but there was little to report. A tentative arrangement was made for Tommy to visit sometime the following week.

When Katie cycled up, Robert was working from a roof ladder on Murphy's cottage.

'Oh, I see you got a high up job now.

What are you doing there?'

'I'm just taking off moss with this wire brush I picked up in Murphy's', he answered, holding the brush up for her to see.

'I suppose you got the ladders there as well'

'I did surely, and I have to have them back first thing in the morning'.

Heavy rain-laden clouds loomed threateningly overhead.

'You'll be lucky to get another hour dry'.

Robert turned his head skywards and was quick to agree with her weather forecasting.

Katie eased her bicycle up against the sidewall and observed something Robert seemed to have missed.

'Come here and look at this'.

Robert slowly made his way down to her with a puzzled look.

'What's up, Love?'

Katie pointed to painted lettering of about two feet in height scrawled on the Abbey side of the wall.

'*British soldiers out'*.

Robert angrily spat out on the ground alongside him.

'If I get the bastard, I will teach him some respect'.

'I just brought over a bit of *Sunlight* soap, a scrubbing brush and a few cleaning rags for the house. Maybe we could get to work on that'.

'It will take several coats of whitewash to mask that blue paint, but there's no point opening a tin of paint with heavy clouds like those in the sky', Katie added.

It wasn't long until the first drops of rain began to fall. Robert was forced to get off the ladder and make his way indoors where the kettle was coming to a boil.

Katie took one look at his rain-spattered shirt, congratulating herself on her weather forecasting.

She washed her hands and dried them in an old tea towel. It was now time to butter some scones she had made earlier in the day. The rain was now rattling off the roof. It sounded as if thousands of pebbles were being flung onto it from above.

In a rare flight of nostalgia, Robert told her that such sounds brought back pleasant childhood memories of being tucked up in bed on wild winter nights.

Katie confessed that, in her childhood, those same sounds frightened her.

'My parents' bedroom was next to mine, and when the heavy rain would start, I would always want to go into their bed. Then, after a few minutes, all three of us would be covered in sweat, but I would feel very safe'.

Robert could not resist the temptation to tease his fiancée.

'So, if this rain keeps up, I might get some company in my bed'.

'Go away, you chancer! You will get more than enough of me in the bed when you put a ring on my finger and make a decent woman of me'.

Robert's need was more urgent.

'But I'm dying for it now, Katie. I'm a young, red-blooded man with needs. I have the full load' he added with an appealing smile.

'The full load! My backside. Will you stop using that awful expression? I told you it's too vulgar'.

'Well, what would you say to a good old feel then? I mean, without the main man making an appearance'.

Katie was growing exasperated by his constant pressing of her to be freer with her favours.

'What is it about men and their animal passions. You are all like roosters in a farmyard. Do you ever think of other things?'

'Of course we do, but are you telling me, Katie Higgins, that women never think about such a thing, that you are all so starched and pure that such a thought never crosses your mind?'

It was not a subject on which she had much information.

'Well, I haven't done a study of this, as you well know. The only girl who ever mentioned this to me was Alice Kelly. I gathered she was keen to get stuck in, only that Edward was dragging the feet as we all learned since'.

Robert was fascinated to hear this. He had never had such an exchange between women being revealed.

'Poor old Edward won't be getting much in the foreseeable future' she surmised.

'Well, I was out there earlier this evening, and I can't say he looked like a man who had got it lately. He definitely has the full load'.

'I told you to stop that', she said firmly, rising to go to the window to check on the cloudburst. The raindrops were hopping six inches off the ground as if they were dancing with rage. The rainwater flowed noisily through the downpipe into the new wooden barrel Robert had bought.

'Just as well, I cleaned out the gutters. It would be some mess otherwise. They might even have given way with the weight'.

'Oh, aren't you the far-seeing young man', Katie teased.

They sat down again and continued to converse. Poor old Gerry was the main topic of conversation between them, but Katie was anxious to hear more about Norah's wedding apparel than Robert was in a position to deliver. Robert's descriptive powers, in this regard were worse than useless. His description might have been as apt for the big top of Duffy's Circus as for his sister's trousseau.

Katie told him that they had a letter from the yanks. They were arriving on Wednesday week, and no preparations were yet in place for them.

'I can do a bit of whitewashing the house and the sheds if you like'.
Robert offered.

'Actually, Joseph started on that this very morning'.

'I hope the whitewash was dry before this downpour'.

'What is this uncle of yours like anyway?'

'Uncle Malachy won't be a problem, but Mother is worried about his wife. You know women are harder to deal with, and at least he knows what he is returning to. Kevin is their son. He must be sixteen or seventeen now. I suppose we can put the uncle and wife in the spare room, and Junior can take the settle bed'.

'How long are you expecting this crowd to stay?'

'About a week, I suppose', she answered.

Robert thought the matter over.

'Katie, do you know what? You can tell your mother that Junior can use the spare bedroom here. I'll give him a bed for a week'.

Katie had not been hinting at this at all, and was thrilled at the kind offer.

'Thank you very much, Robert. You have no idea how grateful my mother will be to you'.

Robert smiled.

'That's the plan. And you, Katie, exactly how grateful are you?'

Katie laughingly dismissed the comment as she strode to the window to have yet another look at the unusually intense downpour. In the distance, rumblings of thunder gathered momentum.

'How on earth am I going to get home in this?'

Robert tried to persuade her to spend the night in the cottage, but even with an offer of a key to lock the bedroom door, Katie insisted on going home.

'Robert, what with my mother expecting me, and she already worried about my father, I just have to go'.

There was no more to be said.

Robert rooted out the oilskin coat he had bought on the fair day.

'Put that on you, and I will give you a bar home'.

'What about my bike? I'll need it to go to work in the Big House in the morning'.

Don't worry about work. I'll drop you up there too'.

'But you'll be back here', she reminded him.

'I don't have to come back here. Can't I sleep on that settle bed you were lining up for the young Yank?'

Katie smiled, rejoicing that her man would put himself out so much for her.

'Robert O' Connor, you are a lifesaver!'

Chapter 29

Katie's mother was sheltering under the stairs clutching a bottle of Holy water. She had a morbid fear of thunder and lightning.

'Oh, thank God, you are safe, Katie. I was worried stiff about you; I thought you might be caught up in the floods'.

'I'm fine, Mother, Robert saw me home on the bar of the bike, and he was good enough to lend me this oilskin. Look how the poor devil is drenched to the skin'.

Robert stood there, his clothes sodden and heavy from the rain. Margaret appreciated this particular act of kindness.

'There is a kind streak in you, Robert, no matter what they say about you'.

'Mother, I wondered if Robert could stay on the settle bed for the night. He's promised to give me a lift to work in the morning before he has to go into the yard'.

Margaret had no problem with that.

'Of course, stay. You wouldn't put a dog out on a night like this'.

With the company, Margaret had mustered up sufficient courage to come out from under the stairs. She took a look at the rain dripping from Robert's clothes before making for her wardrobe to fetch some spare blankets from the top shelf.

Katie was keen to get Robert into dry clothes as soon as possible.

'Robert, get those trousers and jacket off you'.

'Now, you are talking, but are you sure you want to do it with your mother here?'

Katie allowed herself a fleeting smile.

Robert decided against stripping. Instead, he contented himself with standing in front of the open fire.

'Mother, Robert says that Kevin can stay in his cottage when the Yanks arrive'.

Margaret breathed a huge sigh of relief.

'Ah, Robert, that's a weight off my mind. Thank you so much. I have been demented worrying about what to do with the lad. This is only a small house. I can shove the married pair into the spare bed, but you can't throw a big lump of a lad in on top of them'.

'No bother at all. And I hear Gerry is doing well'.

Margaret was not exactly thrilled with her husband's progress.

'He is not too bad, but I have a horrible feeling about the whole thing. Anyway, the good news is he'll be home early next week, and I am counting the hours until I have him back with me', she sighed.

When the family members retired to their rooms for the night, Robert made himself comfortable on the settle bed. The pelting rain on the roof was so loud it delayed his getting to sleep. He tried to picture his Katie, seductively stretched out in her lonesome bed only yards from where he lay. He considered joining her when everyone had settled down but thought better of it. She was unlikely to entertain him and might even create an embarrassing scene.

When sleep eventually came to Robert, Katie could hear his snores from her room. She smiled as she thought.

'So that's what is in store for me!'

Katie was soon sound asleep, as were her brother and mother when Robert sprang upright in the bed at around four o'clock. The battlefield nightmares had followed him to his new resting place. He was bathed in a cold sweat, and his heart was racing mad. It had been one of the most frightening of all his night terrors. He quickly realised that he had also wet his underpants. Luckily, he had disturbed none of the household.

Robert quickly removed the sodden underpants and checked the settle bed. The blanket was slightly damp, but that would not be a problem. He hid his underwear underneath the oilskin and planned to dispose of it in the morning lest anyone see it. He planned to toss it into the hedge as he cycled back to the village. Robert permitted himself a smile as he imagined Gerry and Joseph wondering why any man might toss his drawers into a field. It was worth doing it for that alone.

Chapter 30

Gerry was discharged from the hospital on Tuesday, and the American visitors arrived on the following day. Despite the rather poor timing of the visit, he was looking forward to seeing his brother Malachy after a gap of seven years.

The week spent in a hospital bed had weakened Gerry's muscles, with the result that he struggled to walk. The man did not look well at all. His face was pale, and he had lost some weight. Katie and Margaret constantly fussed over him. He shooed them away as a farmer might an over-excited dog that continued to jump all over him. The doctor had warned Margaret that Gerry was likely to be feeling particularly vulnerable and brittle for several weeks to come. He might imagine that every bit of stray wind in his system was the precursor to a major cardiac event. Gerry had been essentially given a lesson on the fragility of human life.

'I didn't wear no pyjamas last night', Malachy blurted out. It was so damn hot in that boarding house'.

Everyone laughed, but Malachy could not understand the reaction. Gerry and Malachy pulled their chairs closer as Malachy was getting a bit hard of hearing. They chatted earnestly, clutching a glass containing a generous half one of *Jameson* whiskey. Margaret had raised doubts about the advisability of her husband drinking spirits, but Gerry stubbornly refused to toast his brother's visit with water. Katie looked across at the two men and was struck by the extent of the family resemblance. They were like different versions of the same model of Higgins men.

The reunited siblings compared notes on their respective health conditions and the merits of the respective health systems. In recent years, Malachy had developed respiratory problems and was relieved to escape the intense heat of East Coast summers.

'America is a mighty country, but it's all about the dollar. Being sick is a very expensive business for us. In the States, the doctor doesn't feel your pulse until he checks out your wallet first. It might be a great republic, but I say it is still a monarchy because the dollar is King'.

Gerry nodded to indicate that he had got the picture.

'I miss the old country still. Sometimes, I think I might like to move back here, but the winters would kill me', Malachy confessed.

It was Gerry's turn to nod agreement.

'Aye, sure you would miss the home comforts in America', Gerry reckoned.

'I'm sure when you get used to the electric light and the inside toilets, it would be awful tough to go back to the way things were. I bet you'd have to be in some desperate state before you would nip out the back garden on a dark night, and we do that without a second thought'.

Malachy agreed.

'We don't even have a back garden. It's all high-rise apartment buildings in our neighbourhood'.

As the two men chatted, Katie's attention swung between what Susie and her mother discussed and the men's conversation. Whenever she heard her fiancé's name mentioned, that conversation had her undivided attention.

'This young man of Katie's fought in Europe, you tell me, and in the British army too', he added in disbelief.

'Aye, whatever rush of blood to the head he got', her father wondered.

Malachy was a staunch Irish republican who believed that any enemy of England ought to be a friend to Ireland.

'If he had studied the history of our country, he would not have taken the King's Shilling. We saw how the British treated Ireland with the pitch cap and bayonet. Then, you had Cromwell and his butchery. The British spent generations trying to make Protestant Paddies out of us, putting a price on the priest's head. Then, I hear Katie's man fought with a loyalist outfit. How did that go down here in the neighbourhood?'

Gerry told the unvarnished truth about his experience.

'Well, you can imagine, it wasn't popular and still isn't. We won't be let forget it for a long time to come. Some people have not spoken to us since, but the lad himself isn't the worst. Aye, and Katie thinks the world of him, and isn't that what matters in the end?'

Malachy found it difficult to accept.

'There's no accounting for taste'.

'But fighting the Germans! They were fighting the Brits, and from what I recall, the Germans were willing to send guns on Erskine Childers's boat for the Easter Rising?'

'Aye, *The Aud*! Wasn't it, but that didn't get through'.

'No, it didn't because some Paddy spy was doing John Bull's bidding, I suppose. It has always been that way'.

The conversation changed back to talk of old times, so Katie tuned out again.

Her mother was still bravely trying to chat with Susie but was not meeting with much success. It felt like hard work. The lady was a woman of few words. She had to milk every single word out of her.

Katie was deeply upset by her uncle's comments, but the laws of hospitality demanded that she hold her tongue. It was a case of least said, soonest mended. Anyway, she was eavesdropping on a private conversation, and of course, eavesdroppers never hear anything good about themselves.

She was glad that Robert was not there to hear it. He may have been provoked to a bad-tempered response. That would be a recipe for civil war in the Higgins household. Katie knew that her parents disapproved of Robert's actions, and understandably so, but they had consigned that to the past. She shouldn't care what Uncle Malachy thought. He would be gone from them in a few days back to his own life in the USA.

Malachy O' Connor had done well for himself in Philadelphia. He had seemingly amassed a fortune from a combination of hard work and some very good luck when it came to inheritances. Such prosperity was far from the mind of the shy twenty-two-year-old, who had sailed from Queenstown with only a few shillings in his pocket. It must have been a massive cultural shock, going from tending hungry animals on the hillsides of sparsely populated North Leitrim to the bustling city life of America's East coast.

Theodore Roosevelt was the American president then, but that name might well have been a Music Hall act, for all the young Malachy Higgins knew.

This shy young man spent the first few days of the Atlantic crossing, silently enduring the misery of seasickness. Feeling lonely and homesick, he summoned the courage to initiate a conversation with an equally forlorn looking girl he had previously seen on deck. The girl was Susie McGee from County Longford. She, too, was bound for Philadelphia and, eventually bound to be Mrs Malachy Higgins. Malachy and Susie had exchanged the addresses of their respective lodgings. When he had settled in, he came looking for the girl with the lost look in her eyes. They established and maintained contact through the Irish American associations, County Associations and the like, eventually marrying five years later. For some time, it looked as if their marriage was not to be blessed with children, but along came a son, whom they christened Kevin and their world soon revolved around him.

Chapter 31

Seventeen-year-old Kevin Higgins was the first guest to stay over in Robert's spare bedroom. Robert feared that Kevin might well be a moody young American who might have an issue with staying in an isolated cottage on the edge of a graveyard with no running water, electricity or toilet facilities.

He could not have been more wrong.

When he arrived, Kevin did not so much burst into the cottage as much as explode into it. All six foot four of him had the welcome of the day for himself as he arrived, sport's bag in hand, in the company of his Irish cousin, Katie. The young man was built like a tank, and when he spoke, it was in a confident and self-assured manner.

'Hi there, Robert, I'm Kevin, and I am so thrilled to be here', he said, bestowing on Robert the firmest handshake he had ever received.

'This place is truly amazing, Man. I'm told you back onto the cemetery. I've got to see that'.

'Yea, Kevin, we are in the dead centre of Dromahair'.

Kevin laughed heartily at his play on words.

'Hey, you are a funny guy. You should be on the stage. It leaves in five minutes'.

This was a new expression for Robert and left him slightly confused. Everything was amazing to Kevin's eyes. His genuine enthusiasm and his readiness to muck in immediately endeared him to Robert. Katie left after a moment or two of rather stilted small talk and returned home.

'Robert, look after Kevin and keep him out of harm's way. We'll see you tomorrow.'

'And Kevin, you have a good rest after your long journey. Robert will let you have a good lie in. I think that your parents plan to meet you around twelve in the hotel'.

'Thanks, Katie, I think that I am going to be just dandy here'.

Robert half hoped that Katie might stay but understood why she had to rush off.   The thought of entertaining this young man was not something he was looking forward to. It could be a long night in the cottage.

Kevin looked older than his years and this made Robert think that perhaps, he could still go to the bar that night. The young lad was not exactly a child. Of course, Katie would be angry if she found out, but with a bit of luck no one need know anything. It would pass the night and maintain his sanity into the bargain.

Not alone had Kevin no problem with this, he was virtually licking his lips in anticipation.

'Great, wait till I tell my buddies that I drank booze in a real Irish bar'.

Robert would have preferred if Kevin didn't mention this.

'Don't tell your parents, not while you are this side of the Atlantic anyway. And on your sweet Yankee life, don't tell Katie.

Kevin was game for the pub but was anxious to explore his surroundings before drinking.

He was particularly interested in seeing the Higgins family plot in the adjacent graveyard.

As they stuck their noses out of the door, Kevin returned to get his heavy sweater.

'There is a definite chill out there, Robert'.

Robert waited in shirtsleeves while Kevin pulled an extra-large, orange coloured sweater over his head.

'Well, we'll be seen anyway', Robert joked.

In a few steps, the two lads had reached the burial spot of Kevin's paternal ancestors. The young man's appearance took on a more solemn aspect as he stood silently reading from the headstone.

'If only they could know that their grandson from Philadelphia came to visit them'.

The emotion of the moment was not lost on Robert.

He felt uncomfortable as if he was, in some way, encroaching on a very private and special moment. He had not anticipated such reverence.

'Amazing too, we are of this place, and poverty and emigration pushed our people out when they all would have preferred to remain here', he claimed.

Robert felt that America had been good to those emigrants.

'Look what emigration has done for you, lad and your family. You have a far better time in America or do you see that?'

Kevin was circumspect on that point.

'Sure, we have our electricity, our fridge freezers and our fancy stores, but our parents would never have swapped this place for material possessions if they could have made a living in the country they loved'.

Robert allowed Kevin the time to stroll around and survey the adjacent headstones.

The young American had a great feel for the history and was in his element as he tried to visualise where the high altar would have been situated and took in the views that these medieval friars would have taken in each morning.

'You know, Robert, the view from this place would hardly have changed since those days', he added in astonishment.

'Come on, Kevin, enough of the maudlin talk. I need a good drink after this'.

Robert walked on towards the gateway while Kevin continued to soak up the atmosphere in the last resting place of his ancestors.

'I would like to get another look at the village if you wouldn't mind'.

'No bother at all, we'll walk this way so'.

In answer to a question about employment opportunities, Robert gave him an outline account of how he had planned to go to London for a year or so, amass a small fortune and return to live the life of a lord in the town.

'But Katie knocked that on the head, I guess'.

'You guessed right. She even told me she would not be waiting for me when I returned'.

'I can imagine that she must have burst your bubble then, Rob?'

Robert smiled at the manner in which his name was abbreviated. Nobody in the village had ever referred to him as Rob.

'That she did, Kevin, that she did, but I would have thought that she might have jumped at the prospect of a little nest egg being built up'.

'Maybe she loves you a little bit more than she loves money. And, after all, you had been away for a couple of years in the military'.

'Yea, but it's not as if I enlisted for enjoyment'.

'Well, true, Rob, but I am sure she counted the days till God sent you back safe to her. The last thing she would have wanted was you to abandon her again.'

Robert shook his head defiantly.

'Ah, sure, there's no point in talking to you. You are only echoing what she said'.

'My dad can't understand how you have enlisted in the Crown Forces. He sees the Brits as the old enemy, and you were seen to let the side down'.

Robert gave a mocking laugh.

'I'm not a bit surprised, sure my father was horrified by it and to make matters worse, I went with what was seen as a sectarian regiment. When I finally croak it, I don't think I'll be buried in a Republican Plot.'

'The Protestants won't want you either. I can tell you,' Kevin ventured.

Robert feigned insult.

Listen here, Yankee Doodle Kevin, less cheek out of you, or you'll be sleeping out with the bones of your ancestors tonight, with only that awful orange jumper on you for warmth.

'I told you we would get on', Kevin laughed as if he gave Robert a playful yet powerful slap on the back.

'Come on, I will introduce you to the attractions of our nearest saloon bar'.

Chapter 32

Robert led the way into the public bar of the hotel. Two vacant stools stood at the side of the bar. The two lads plonked themselves down as Kevin licked his lips in anticipation.

The barman welcomed both.

'John, this is my American friend. Give us two stouts and keep them coming'.

'Is your friend the legal age for drinking in this country?'

'Does he look as if he is a child to you?' Robert replied.

The barman shrugged his shoulders.

'Well, he looks more a man than anyone here'.

Robert threw his eye around the bar room. The usual suspects were in position.

When the drinks were delivered, Kevin savoured each mouthful of his drink, as if he were memorising everything for a thesis on the sensual pleasures of a pint of porter.

'So, my friend, you tell me that you are looking for a girlfriend? It would help if you had a type in mind', Robert suggested.

'Ideally, I want an Irish colleen, like my cousin, Katie, but I might be out of luck there'.

'Well, there's only one Katie Higgins, but we could negotiate if the price is right', he joked.

'My advice to you, Kevin, is to play the field. Do you understand that expression?'

'You mean I should sow my wild oats before settling down with one girl'.

Despite the confident exterior, Kevin was an insecure young man who was eager to learn about life. He would take advice from anyone with experience in the romantic field.

He was keen to hear how Robert met his cousin Katie.

'Oh, I met her at a dance in the parish hall. It was an *Excuse Me* dance. I moved in'.

Kevin looked confused.

'Now, you have got to explain that to me'.

Robert explained that it was a dance where other men were permitted to cut in and continue the dance with that girl.

'Sounds like a recipe for a whole lot of trouble'.

'Not really, they generally passed off peacefully enough. Well, I cut in on the bloke Katie was dancing with. Naturally, she couldn't resist me, and as they say, the rest is history. Our wedding is planned for sometime in October'.

'So, there's no definite date set yet'.

'It depends on the priest's retreat dates, but I am just after writing off for my letter of freedom'.

Kevin screwed up his face again.

'What the heck is that?'

Once explained, he had no difficulty understanding what a letter of freedom was.

'And what attracted you to Cousin Katie?'

'You ask more questions than a parish priest in a confessional'.

'Sorry, Robert, but I am intrigued because I am a novice in the area'.

Robert understood and was not in the least bothered. He sipped from his glass and thought for a moment.

'It was her good looks, I suppose, but there is a thing called attraction or chemistry. You are helplessly drawn to that person'.

'Right then', he mused. 'That must be what the books term 'sexual attraction'.

'And you felt that attraction towards Katie'.

Robert winked at Kevin before answering.

'No, I didn't. I was telling you that there was such a thing'.

Kevin did not know what to believe.

Robert finished his drink and ordered two more.

'You are very mature for seventeen. When I was seventeen, I was a total innocent and never knew anything beyond a four-mile radius of here'.

Kevin found it difficult to keep up with Robert in knocking the drinks back. The taste of the porter did not appeal to him, but he presumed that it was an acquired taste. In his mind, any self-respecting son of Erin had to persist until he developed a taste for the black stuff.

When Kevin rose to go to the toilet, he staggered and nearly fell over the stool he had been sitting on. This was Robert's first indication that the novice had greatly exceeded his capacity.

Robert was angry with himself for allowing this to happen. The last thing he wanted was to have a drunken Kevin staggering around the hotel and tripping himself up in the town's streets. Katie would kill him and her family would always resent him for his reckless endangerment of one of their own.

He had to get Kevin home as quickly as possible.

Grabbing the big lad by the arm, Robert linked the young man onto the street. The river walk was mercifully close, so he could quickly move him away from prying eyes. Kevin complained that he needed to go to the toilet, but Robert dragged him under the trees, insisting that he do his business there.

This experience was a novelty for the young American.

'Wow, this is savage man! I am actually taking a leak under an Irish ash tree, belly full of black porter and ready to spend the night in a cottage on the edge of a cemetery. Man, but there is definitely a book in this'.

Eventually, Robert managed to get Kevin back to the cottage by a mixture of pulling and dragging. Kevin fell through the open door and desperately made for the safety of one of the kitchen chairs.

'Help me, Man, the room is spinning around me'.

Robert scratched his head, wondering what he should do. Morning must not find him with a hangover and the stink of vomit on his clothing.

Robert opened the back door and dragged Kevin outside, where he suggested that Kevin short circuit the sobering up process by making himself sick rather than wait for it to happen naturally over his clothes or onto the bed.

'Come on, Kevin, it will bring up all that porter that's weighing heavily on your belly. After that, you will feel a lot better'.

Kevin was adamant.

'I'm not going to shove my finger down my throat or anywhere else for that matter. You got that, Robert?'

Robert had got no such thing.

He opted for the direct route, grabbing the young man around the neck as he had often done with cattle when dosing them. Before Kevin could utter a word, Robert rammed his finger down his young friend's throat. Almost immediately, the contents of his stomach spewed out all over the grass.

'Hey man, have you gone nuts altogether? I thought you were my friend'.

'I am your friend, and only a friend would do that. You'll be thanking me for it later'.

Kevin had to admit that he was already feeling a little bit better. The feeling of nausea was on the wane, and his balance seemed to be improving. The cottage had stopped spinning, but he felt exhausted and wanted to collapse into bed.

Robert was not finished yet. Years of drinking experience had taught him something. He filled a mug with water from the bucket near the door.

'Now, you are not going to any bed until you drink two full mugs of water. That should make sure you have no bad hangover in the morning'.

'I suppose you will pour it down my throat if I refuse', Kevin complained bitterly.

'Got it in one, Man, as you say. Down your throat or up your arse, you decide. I am going to get it into you one way or another'.

'Hey, Robert, you are a truly hideous creature. I can't see why my cousin would ever want to marry a ruffian like you'.

'Cos she loves me', Robert replied. 'Because she loves me, and she can't help it'.

Kevin might have been a fair bit the worse for wear, but he was still interested in the subject of relationships.

'Did you worry about her dating another man when you were away on the battlefront?'

'I didn't, but I probably should have. I was too bloody complacent'.

'And if she had gone with another, would you have any idea of the type she would be attracted to?'

'Well, it's funny the questions you think to ask'.

I'd imagine she'd go for the one who was most like me. So, to answer your question, I'd say she'd have ended up chasing my father'.

Despite his discomfort, Kevin could not help laughing.

'You're funny, cousin Bob. You're crazy too but you are so funny'.

Kevin finished both mugs of water even though it took him almost half an hour to do so. Taking so much water necessitated two trips outside before he was ready for the bed.

Robert assisted him to the spare bedroom and removed his shoes and what clothes he could manage. He then pulled the quilt over him. To be on the safe side, Robert advised the young American to lie on his side, lest he choke on his vomit during the night.

'Goodnight, Kevin! I'll see you in the morning.'

'Not if I see you first, you mad man you'.

Robert need not have worried about how Kevin might be in the morning. During the night, Gerry Higgins had died in his sleep. The whole house was in a state of confusion and the excesses of the previous night mattered little.

Chapter 33

After Margaret Higgins discovered her husband cold in the bed beside her, there was a constant flow of people coming and going. The priest and the doctor had been summoned. Both had been so comforting and supportive, but it was all so surreal for Margaret. Luckily, the remains did not have to be removed from the house for a post mortem. Dr Clarke certified that the deceased had an underlying heart condition and had died from a massive heart attack. Robert heard the sad news when he was getting dressed for work. Kevin was up like a light once he became aware of his uncle's death. Any hangover that he may have had was short-lived, as he was determined to get to the wake house in the shortest time possible. Robert was in a hurry there too. He wanted to be there for Katie, but first, he needed to call on his employer and explain why he would not be at work that morning.

Robert had intended putting Kevin on the bar of the bike and cycling over to Katie's, but the lad was too big and bulky for that. The only solution was to have Kevin do the cycling with Robert sitting on the bar.

This was a new one for him. He realised they must have cut a strange sight on the road that morning.

Mr Murphy could not have been more understanding. He was shocked at the tragic news and considered the deceased as much a friend as a customer.

'Robert, you are practically family there. You have to be with Katie. Take the day off and try to help the poor widow also. She must be distraught'.

Robert agreed to come in the following morning and finish early, presuming the removal was on Friday evening. He would also have to attend the funeral.

'You will not lose any pay, but I know that you will make up for it on your return.

'You have my word on that, Mr Murphy'.

The door of the Higgins house was open. The morning sun reflected off the recently applied whitewash as Robert and Kevin cycled up the laneway. They were greeted first by Katie's brother, Joseph, whose eyes were red from crying.

'Come here to me, Joseph lad. I am so sorry for your trouble'. Kevin hugged his first cousin and patted him comfortingly on the shoulder.

The corpse had been laid out in the front bedroom. Margaret was standing by her husband's deathbed, supported by her daughter Katie and her sister-in-law, Susie. Mother and daughter were already dressed in black. They held handkerchiefs to their eyes in a vain attempt to stifle the constant river of tears that flowed from them. Katie embraced Robert as he sympathised with her. She clung to him in the hope that some small crumb of comfort could be garnered from doing so. Robert could feel the warm tears on his shoulder as they soaked through his light summer shirt. He would have loved to whisper words of comfort, but he could think of none. Instead, he just held her.

He also reached out a hand to Margaret, who grabbed it and clutched it to her.

'Robert, what are we going to do without Gerry? How will we manage at all?'

Robert felt his own eyes well up with sadness.

'We'll have to do our very best and stick together as well as we can. That would be what Gerry would have wanted'.

Robert wished he could have said something more meaningful.

Anxious to get out of the house, Katie took Robert on a walk down the laneway that led to the road. She sobbed bitterly, but she was keen to talk.

'We were so grateful and relieved when he was discharged from the hospital. Our hopes were high, and we allowed ourselves to hope. The poor man, he died without any of us knowing. The doctor said that he most likely died in his sleep'.

'That was nice for him, Katie, but an awful shock for all of you'.

It certainly was a great shock.

A little up the laneway they met her Uncle Malachy. He needed to clear his head and had taken to the outdoors. Katie introduced him to Robert.

'I am pleased to meet you, Malachy. Katie has spoken a lot about you. And I want you to know that I am sorry for your trouble'.

'I know that lad. It's a terrible blow, but I am grateful that God directed me to come here yesterday and meet up with my brother before he passed away. You know, Robert, he was younger than I. He wasn't even sixty. There were years in him only for the heart trouble'.

'At least he had such a peaceful passing', Robert said, struggling to clutch at any straw of comfort.

'So, you are the soldier, laddie. You caused quite a bit of a stir when you enlisted. That was an odd move'.

'I know, Malachy. It wasn't an impulsive thing. I felt I had to do something. Neutrality is understandable for a new state, but the Nazis needed to be beaten', he stated.

'I don't doubt your sincerity, but I think you were misguided. The British have done unspeakable acts in this country, even this parish'.

Robert was indignant, but out of respect for Katie and the tragic occasion, he chose not to exacerbate the situation by challenging the older man.

Katie felt embarrassed by her uncle's truculent attitude, but she was proud of her fiancé's diplomatic response.

'I'm so sorry, Robert. Malachy is in no way diplomatic'.

'Don't you give it a moment's thought. It doesn't matter, especially now'.

The pair walked along together as far as the crossroads, about a half a mile away.

Katie spoke about Gerry. Her emotions were all confused. She cried, she laughed, and she cried again. She shouted, and she whispered. She hugged Robert, and she punched him, angry from her grief. Having sat on the bridge and looked at the water beneath, she was forced to think of how life would be different from here on. Like with the stream, life would continue to flow, but it would not be the same water. Life would go on, but Gerry was gone, and he would not be coming back to them.

She knew how much her mother would miss Gerry. He had been the love of her life, the man she chose as a life partner. Katie would miss her father enormously, but this empty feeling in the pit of her stomach would pass. Robert was the love of her life. She considered herself fortunate that she still had him by her side.

 They walked back to what was now a wakehouse. Neighbours had arrived to sympathise and assure the family that they were all sorry for their trouble. Gerry was a very quiet, popular man and people were genuinely sorry that he had passed away.

They were also shocked that a man who seemed so fit and active a couple of weeks ago had suddenly been stilled by death. Joseph had been dispatched to the village to purchase supplies of drink for the wake. Neighbours brought sandwiches, buns and tarts. Two neighbour women had put the corpse overboard, meaning they prepared the corpse for the funeral.

The wake was already on and would continue until the removal to the church on Friday evening. Numerous pots of tea would be served, countless sandwiches eaten, cigarettes smoked, and alcohol drunk. The deceased's life would be celebrated, and his death mourned in almost equal measure.

After a couple of hours, Robert grew weary of everything and decided to return to his job.

'I wasn't expecting to see you here today, Robert. How is the family bearing up?'

'They are doing their best, Mr Murphy, but it hasn't registered with them yet'.

'Yes, it's not till the crowds go and you are left on your own that it hits one'.

The yard had been quiet all morning, but business had begun to take up a bit.

'It's like they knew you were back, Robert', Mr Murphy joked.

Robert was glad to have somewhere to go. The wake house was boring him to death, sitting there reciting the same thing repeatedly to different people. Katie and her family were stuck there, but he wasn't. He had told Joseph that he would be back later and do the all-night shift. He hoped that Katie and her mother might get some sleep, but he doubted it. The doctor had offered them sleeping tablets, but both had declined his offer.

At around ten-thirty, Robert returned to the wake house. The stream of callers had slowed down. Only a handful of close neighbours, friends and family remained. Katie was thrilled to see him return.

'How are you since?' Robert asked.

'Ah, much the same, dry in the mouth from talking. I had not figured on so many people calling'.

'Your father was well-liked, and a sudden death always brings out a crowd'.

'By the way, your brother Edward called around seven o'clock'.

'Did he now? And what had he to say?'

'Well, the usual: 'Sorry for your trouble', and he even gave me a hug'.

'I see, and what was the form like with him?'

'He seemed genuinely sorry, and there was no other talk about anything. I hope he's getting over all that nonsense'.

'Maybe he is, and maybe he's not. Mother says he still skips off and never says where he is going'.

'Maybe he's seeing someone?'

'I wouldn't think so. I talked to Alice about the dance in the Manor Hall last week. She said Edward was there, but he didn't seem interested in dancing. He was more mooching around the back of the hall'.

Robert urged Katie to get her head down for a while, but she told him that it would be a waste of time for another couple of hours anyway. However, she promised to try to tempt her mother to bed. By midnight both ladies had retired to their rooms, but nobody was betting on them getting any sleep. Meanwhile, in the kitchen, the drink was flowing as the stories were being told. Malachy had livened up considerably. The whiskey seemed to have lubricated his vocal cords. He told jokes and stories that he had picked up in the States.

Laughter filled the kitchen as it did on many occasions during the long night. One could be forgiven for forgetting that it was a wake house, but that was generally how the long nights passed. Young Kevin could not believe what he was witnessing. He could not tell whether it was a musical session, a story telling festival or an all-night mourning ritual.

'I guess I'm just experiencing an Irish wake'.

Inevitably, the conversation would flow back to talk of the deceased and the fine man he had been. The hours passed, and soon dawn broke in the Eastern sky.

Chapter 34

After the burial, the Higgins family returned home. It was a very poignant occasion with precious few words spoken. Margaret plopped lifelessly down in her armchair by the fire, looking forlornly at the empty chair on the other side of the fireplace. That chair would be forever empty. She wondered how she could acquire the strength to face each day, knowing that her beloved Gerry was gone.

Margaret had always been a woman of great faith, but the notions of Christian consolation and the joy of the Resurrection were much too philosophical to be of any benefit right now. All she knew was there would be no Gerry when she would go to bed that night, no Gerry when she would wake up in the morning, no Gerry to share the bad times with or celebrate the good times.

Katie, too, had to accept that her father would never be there for her again. His quiet but hugely influential presence in the home would be no more. He would not be there to walk her up the aisle on her wedding day. That realisation made her so sad.

It then dawned on her that the wedding would have to be postponed as a mark of respect to her late father. The next few months would be like a period of mourning for Robert too. He and Katie might well have attended their last dance together. The usual practice was that when a close family member died, the family would immediately go into mourning for a period of up to twelve months.

The bereaved family would not send Christmas cards that year, and they would not attend any weddings either. Family weddings, if already arranged, would be postponed for some months or limited to smaller gatherings with no music or dance. The prospect of living like a monk the next twelve months did not appeal to Robert.

Much to her distaste, Katie suggested postponing the wedding until the following summer, but Robert felt that early spring might be a better time. To Katie, it was a matter of respect and under no circumstances could she be coaxed down the aisle until at least six months had elapsed. She was looking forward to married life, but she was not going to disrespect her late father's memory. Still, Katie also wanted to be fair to Robert. She appreciated that he was hurting and felt cheated by the turn of events.

A couple of weeks after Gerry's death, Katie talked it through with her mother. Margaret had no objection to the couple tying the knot early in 1947. The wedding day would be a bitter/sweet day, but she assured her daughter that Gerry would be looking down on her as her brother, Joseph, led her up the aisle.

They checked the calendar for suitable dates. Lent was out, so it was a straight choice of before Lent or after Easter. Robert opted for the earlier option, but he left the choice of date up to Katie. She needed little time to decide.

Friday, February 14, was settled on. It was the Feast of St. Valentine, the patron saint of lovers. That date seemed appropriate to her. Katie was very reluctant to leave her mother's side in the first few weeks after Gerry's death.

Not until the Month's Mind Mass was over in early August did she even visit Robert in his cottage. He always had to come to her. The couple might chat and take the odd stroll together, but this was not to Robert's liking. Yet another letter arrived from his friend, Billy Parkes, in London. Once again, he gave a typically upbeat account of the labour market there and the truly amazing social life.

The letter rekindled Robert's earlier desire to work in London for some months. In his mind, this period of inactivity might be the ideal time to work away from home. He could return with the means to make life much more comfortable for Katie and himself.

When he was not seeing Katie, Robert would sometimes nip into one of the pubs for a few drinks. He was supposed to be saving money, but it was difficult to be disciplined after life delivered you a good kick in the teeth. He felt cheated that he was not earning big money in London and enjoying a great social life. He also resented that Katie was spending her evenings at home with her family and being unavailable to him when he needed her.

For one or two days, he toyed with the idea of trying to persuade Katie to agree to his going to England, even until after Christmas. His decision not to resurrect the divisive proposal was down to advice from Alice Kelly. The pair had grown closer since Gerry Higgins's death. Apart from the occasional chats over lunch, Alice often called down to the cottage in the evening. Robert looked forward to her company. Cycling out to Katie's house had almost become a chore. In those early weeks, Katie had not been her usual self. There was not the usual sparkle to her.

The conversation would invariably turn to Gerry, and Robert had grown tired of the mournful double act that was Katie and her mother.

'This time last month, Gerry was coming home from hospital' or 'The last time we bought coal, Daddy carried it into the house.'

While it was all very understandable, and Robert sympathised with them, he longed for the day when this pall of grief would lift and he could get his old Katie back.

It was equally understandable why Robert looked forward to Alice's occasional visits.

Despite the knockback she had suffered, she showed her resilience. She even traced how things had gradually petered out between Edward and her.

'He was so bloody slow about doing anything. I wanted to set a date for our wedding, but he always came up with some excuse to postpone things.'

She had attended recent dances and had met a few new young men. She reported how she felt about the various boys whom she met at local dances. She would score them all out of ten under three headings.

She joked that those headings were: looks, appearance and physical attractiveness.

'Those are the same things, Alice'.

She laughed heartily.

'I know they are. Looks are very important to me in case you have not guessed it already'.

Robert was glad to see that she was in good form again and that she seemed to have his brother out of her system.

Robert also treated Alice as a confidante. He confessed his frustration over the postponement of the wedding. The mournful and depressing atmosphere in the Higgins's house was getting to be too much for him. Often, he would be relieved if there were some excuse not to visit.

'I often feel like shaking them and telling them that Gerry is dead. Get that into your heads. The rest of you are still alive, so live life. Is that so terrible, Alice?'

Alice was very disappointed at his attitude and did not offer him the response he had expected.

'Yes, it is terrible, and you are so selfish. Katie and her family are going through a terrible period of mourning. You know well, they can't be all singing and all dancing. Imagine that you were to die in thirty or forty years, leaving Katie a widow and her children fatherless. What would you think if Katie was all smiles, meeting and greeting the people? Wouldn't there be something unnatural in that?'

Robert could understand that but was reluctant to admit it.

'It wouldn't bother me any if I were dead'.

'Furthermore, Robert O' Connor, what would you think of a randy, young fellow being mad with your daughter because she hadn't snapped out of the grief in three or four weeks?'

'I would give that selfish bastard a kick in the arse out of the place'.

'And right you would be'.

Robert liked that Alice was so frank and so direct with him. She also had a lively personality that appealed to him, and as regards looks, she would certainly be an eight on her one-to-ten scale.

'Alice Kelly, I hope you take this in the spirit I intend, but if I had not met Katie, I would have chanced my luck with you', he admitted.

'You might think that, but I would not be as keen. Don't you think that I would have enough of the O' Connor men after Edward, without taking on his younger brother?'

She had a point.

'Definitely, you'd want to be a right glutton for punishment. We must be two of the most selfish bastards in the county'.

'Well, you are probably up there with the worst of them anyway'.

Robert was suddenly curious about a related topic.

'Tell me this, Alice, if I were a stranger and you had met me at the dance, how would I have fared under your three headings?'

Alice coyly turned her face away from him and answered in total honesty.

'Nine out of ten in all three, she replied, her face beginning to redden with embarrassment.

Robert was flattered but feigned insult.

'Hey, where did I lose the mark?'

'You lost the mark, because you failed to notice me first', she answered.

Now, it was Robert's turn to be embarrassed.

The conversation had got more personal than he, or even she, could have anticipated. To hear such sentiment expressed was both flattering and disconcerting in equal measure. He was tempted to hold her in his arms and feel her heartbeat excitedly alongside his. They were, after all, two lonely people, cruelly frustrated in their desire for love. His body needed loving. His soul needed comforting, but to do anything about it would not alone be a mistake, it would be an act of selfishness and betrayal. Robert drew back in his chair and regretfully shook his head.

'We could ruin everything, everything good between us', he said.

Alice looked uncomfortable. She seemed not to know whether she should feel embarrassed, rejected, or even respected. In her own way, she felt that her moment of weakness had passed without real damage being done.

'Robert, I know we would be making a whole bagful of trouble for ourselves, but there are times when you need to grab whatever is on offer. Playing by the rules has not done me any good this far anyway. Being messed around by two O' Connors was not what I needed.'

'Or the priest either', she laughed.

'Ah, to hell with all of it ', said Robert. 'Come here to me till I give you a squeeze'.

Alice flung herself into his arms and clung tight for all she was worth. There was reassurance as well as pleasure in that closeness to him.

She was unwilling to let go, and for a minute, at least, the two held that embrace in the middle of the dimly lit kitchen. Robert finally moved to break from the embrace, but Alice clung on for all she was worth. He moved his head back a little and looked her straight in the eye.

Despite his earlier taking the high moral ground, the long embrace had greatly increased the desire within him. Robert's moral compass was found wanting. It failed miserably to keep his physical desires in check. Before one could say 'Katie Higgins', Alice and he had divested themselves of their clothing. Their naked young bodies soon lay together on Robert's unmade bed. They hungrily pleasured each other, enthusiastically making up for lost time and recent frustrations.

For the first time in ages, Robert felt human again. There certainly was pleasure in this world, and he had no regrets about having grabbed some of it when it was offered to him. He presumed from her self-satisfied expression that Alice felt the same way, but she did not articulate that.

'You don't know how much I needed that, Alice'

'Not nearly as much as I needed it', she replied

'Christ, I always thought you were a well-reared, decent girl'.

'Well, it just shows you can be very wrong about people'.

Robert climbed out of bed and set about getting dressed again. After a moment or two of bemused head shaking, Alice did likewise. They returned to the kitchen when they were both dressed and sat down.

'Maybe we should not have done that, but it was a real treat, Alice, thank you.

'You are most welcome, kind Sir, but don't thank me, sure we just used each other for our pleasure, and that's all. There is nothing more to it'.

Robert was relieved that Alice had not shown signs of getting clingy. That would be the last thing he would have wanted.

'We must do it again sometime', he ventured.

'Somehow, I don't think you will be feeling like that again soon. If you have any conscience in you, you will regret what you did behind poor old Katie Higgins's back'.

Robert felt that Alice might well be correct in that prediction.

She had no such misgivings about hurting Katie.

'Katie Higgins is no friend of mine. She thinks she's so bloody great with the two O' Connor brothers sniffing around her'.

Sometimes, the prevailing mood can change suddenly, and Robert detected a degree of bitterness entering the conversation. This quickly became a passion killer and the first indication of a problem brewing for him.

Alice got distracted when she noticed the transformation of the cottage.

'You have a lot done with it, a lot of nice little shelves and trinkets'.

'Thanks, Alice, I robbed those out of the yard unknown to the boss, but don't whisper that around Murphy's'.

'Robert O' Connor, I am shocked to think that you would bite the hand that feeds you. What sort of a person does that make you?'

'Well, he has the value of them out of me. Anyway, they are only improving his cottage'.

'I suppose', she replied in a resigned tone.

'But it's a lovely snug little place, a romantic place and what about you getting married on St. Valentine's Day. How romantic is that? It's like something you would see in the picture house'.

'It's a day like any other too, I suppose, but it won't be the big wedding Katie had been planning. It will be a smaller do. You know, with Gerry kicking the bucket so recently and all'.

'Does that bother you?'

'No, I never gave a monkeys about the wedding. I want to marry Katie, and I don't care how big or small the occasion is.

'Aw, isn't that so touching from the lovely groom to be. Tell me now, where will the breakfast be?'

'*The Imperial Hotel* in Sligo, the same spot where Norah's wedding will be'.

'I need to know these things for when I snare a good man for myself.'

'Good men are hard to find Alice. There are not many like me around.'

Alice shook her head.

'You might be great between the sheets, but I doubt that you are husband material. A wife would never know where you might have been'.

Robert was indignant.

'That's a bit Irish coming from you after what you have just been doing. Sure, any poor husband might feel that you would always be liable to break out like some young heifer in heat'.

Being compared to a dumb animal was highly insulting, and only served to worsen her mood.

'Vows mean something to me, if you must know, and I have a spiritual side if you hadn't noticed.

'Have you now, Miss High and Mighty? And what spiritual reasons did you have for hopping into bed with me?'

The atmosphere had completely soured in seconds.

'Maybe I had, and maybe I just took pity on you. Who said that you are that great anyway?'

'You did'.

'I was only being nice to you in case I might hurt your feelings'.

'Well, tell me where I am coming up short?' he demanded.

'Right then, seeing as you asked. You are totally selfish. It's always about you and what you want. Your fiancée was going through hell, and all you could think about was your pleasure. Before that, you joined the British army, knowing that it would embarrass everyone belonging to you, and you did not care. It will always be what Robert wants. Does that answer your question?'

'I'm sorry I asked. I thought you liked me'.

'Like you? You will do, I suppose, for a bit of slap and tickle. I like your company. I suppose your chat and body are attractive, by the standards of this place, but I wouldn't marry you if you were the last man in the county, no insult intended now'.

'Insult taken', Robert snapped. 'I think it's time you went home now, Miss Kelly'.

'Right, see you tomorrow at work, Mister O' Connor'.

Chapter 35

Alice's visits to the isolated cottage grew more infrequent. Her relationship with Robert had cooled significantly. Conversations between them became more stilted and infrequent. Robert was left in little doubt that Alice regretted their moments of passion.

Alice's prior visits might have been discreet, but they had not gone unnoticed in the village. One morning, as Katie was absentmindedly wheeling her bicycle, well laden down with shopping bags, she encountered a brazen Edward O' Connor. He had been loitering in the area for some considerable time with the hope of meeting her.

'How are you now, Katie. How's the heart?'

He spoke with a studied calmness.

A nervous Katie politely thanked him for his enquiry and assured him that her heart was just fine and she was learning to cope better with the loss of her father.

Edward was uncharacteristically philosophical and sympathetic.

'One day, you will waken and the pain will be less. Then, you will realise that you can pick up the threads of your life again'.

Although Edward had mouthed those words, they were not truly his. Katie wondered where he had read or heard those sentiments. Either way, she felt sure that he had rehearsed them.

'And I hear the wedding is not going ahead in October', he added, his demeanour suggesting that this was less of a casual remark than a conversation starter.

'Yes, we put the date back, with the funeral and all. We couldn't be all dressed up and smiling when our hearts were breaking'.

'No, you couldn't, but there is generally some heartbreak at a wedding. I would imagine'.

Katie sensed that she was being led down a road she did not wish to travel. She attempted to excuse herself, citing her busy schedule, but Edward seemed insistent. He seemed to have his lines prepared and knew when to deliver them.

'It's tough on Robert too. I mean, it's no fun when your fiancée has little time for you with all her commitments elsewhere. You can't blame the man for feeling a bit abandoned'.

This was far from being a throwaway remark, and it made Katie perk up and take notice. Perhaps Edward had picked up on some impatience and resentment on his brother's part. However, considering the poor relationship between them, she could be certain that Robert did not confide in his brother. If Edward had heard anything in this vein, it was most likely from his parents.

Edward's eyes told the story. He was a man delivering a performance. His lines had been well rehearsed, and this encounter was anything but a random one. Katie suspected that she had been waylaid and that Edward had been stalking her.

She suspected that he was leading up to something even more disconcerting.

She had not long to wait.

'It's good that Robert had Alice to keep him company when you were busy helping your mother', he said, scanning her face for a reaction. She would have demanded some explanation in any other circumstance, but she was disinclined to give Edward the satisfaction. Her reply was as measured as she could manage.

'It was indeed. Alice is a nice girl, and I think you were foolish to let her go', she chanced as she walked away.

Katie felt sure that her eyes must have betrayed her horror at the suggestion of something going on between Alice and her Robert.

She had no idea what Edward meant, and had no intention of questioning him on that point. Instead, she continued on her route for the moment.

She was determined to quiz Robert on the matter when she next saw him.

Edward had kept one last verbal grenade until he was about thirty yards away from her.

'Maybe Alice might still become Mrs O' Connor'.

Katie let Edward go out of sight before retracing her footsteps in the direction of Main Street. She went in the side gate to Murphy's and immediately caught sight of Robert sawing some timber for a local tradesman. Robert saw her and signalled to her that she should wait a moment.

Mr Murphy had cautioned against social calls during work time, and Katie had little desire to give the man any cause for complaint.

She shouted a brief message to him.

'See you in the cottage at seven'.

Robert smiled and raised an arm to acknowledge the arrangement.

His warm smile and favourable reaction did much to ease her concerns.

As she made her way out of the yard, she heard someone call out to her.

'Trouble brewing, I would say'.

Edward had shadowed her back to the yard. She had been played by her stalker and had done exactly what he hoped she would do. Katie knew that she was dancing to Edward's tune, but was determined that it would never happen again.

Chapter 36

Robert was so pleased to see Katie walking down the pathway to the cottage. Hopefully, it was an indication of a normal relationship being restored between them. He missed the privacy the cottage had offered them. Her house held little attraction as a meeting place. Even without the gloomy atmosphere pervading the place, it was still her family home and no substitute for their own private space.

As she neared the door, he grabbed her, lifted her high in his arms and carried her over the threshold. Katie was delighted at the enthusiasm of the welcome, even if she considered it to be a little excessive.

'Put me down, you fool. It's only when we're married you can do that'.

'Ah, why do all the fun things have to wait until we are married? It's a pity to be always ruled by tradition. Let's do what we bloody well feel like doing and ignore what anyone else thinks'.

Katie did not subscribe to that view.

'Life is not as simple as that. We have to consider other people'.

Katie was glad that she had made the visit. Whether Edward was telling lies or half-truths, she would not make an issue of it. After all, her homestead must have been a depressing place to visit. Ironically, Edward had done her a huge favour. She had a new perspective on life.

Her father was dead.

He wasn't coming back.

No amount of crying or feeling miserable would change that, but Katie had a life to live. Things were different now. Her mother, for one, would need more support than previously, but Katie had other responsibilities and Robert was one of those. She was determined that she would be as much her old self to him as she could be.

When Robert eased her back onto her feet, she put her arms out and embraced him.

'You have been great to keep our relationship going while my mind was elsewhere. You came up to a dreary, depressing house on so many occasions to see me. That's too much to expect of any man. I neglected you since my father's death, but that neglect is coming to an end'.

These sentiments were music to his ears, but he could never have imagined what had brought about the change in her attitude.

'How could a house be anything but miserable only a few weeks after a death?'

'I know that, but it had to be misery for you coming into that atmosphere week after week. I'd say there were times you would have been glad of any excuse to stay away'.

Robert did not attempt to deny the reality of that remark.

'Well, I'd be lying if I said that I always looked forward to it, but I wanted to see you, and if that meant going into that atmosphere, then that's what I was going to do'.

'Robert, thank you for that, and I presume that being stuck here alone couldn't have been a barrel of laughs either. Maybe you had callers'.

'There were very few and some of those I could have done without'.

Katie decided to probe a little more.

'And the ones you looked forward to?'

This was getting a little too close for comfort.

Initially, Robert intended to play the innocent.

'Well, Josie Taylor called in the odd time when he was at a loose end'.

'Did anyone from the shop visit?'

Robert gave her a quizzical look, which had not gone unnoticed by Katie.

He rightly suspected that someone had been stirring up suspicions in her mind. There was no point in denying the facts. He decided to come clean with her.

'Alice Kelly called a few times after work. She thought I needed cheering up'.

The openness of the response pleased Katie, but it was not the sort of thing she wanted to hear.

The thought that a lonely Robert might have been looking forward to Alice's visits, stirred feelings of jealousy in her.

It was high time she got back on the scene and reclaimed exclusive rights to her man.

Katie voiced her suspicions in relation to Edward stalking her.

'I wouldn't think he'd be up to that. He probably saw you and that gave him the idea of following you. Anyway, what had he to say?'

'It was weird. He talked about grief and healing, you know. It was weird stuff especially coming from him'.

'My brother, the philosopher!' he scoffed.

'He was on about death making you reconsider everything. It was so strange'.

Robert agreed that this did not sound like the Edward he was familiar with.

'How did he look?'

'He looked calm enough and normal as any of us, none of the intensity in his eyes, but I didn't like how his mind was working'.

Robert was not unduly worried about the disclosure.

'My mother said he seems to be getting back to himself although he still disappears for ages at a time'.

Robert put the kettle on, and while they were waiting on it to boil, she complimented him on how well the cottage was looking.

'Oh, I gave the inside a lick of paint. It was mainly out of pure boredom. And I had to give the outside a bit of a touch-up in places.'

'Why was that then?'

'Well, that was down to the unwanted callers'.

Katie laughed. She had been so interested in his news about Alice calling that the remark had gone unnoticed. She had noticed the touch-up but presumed it was merely covering up the spattering of liquid cow dung from passing cows.

'It was nothing as innocent as that. Anyway, cow shite would mostly wash off even if I left it to the rain. No, someone came with a pot of blue paint and a brush and painted messages on my walls'.

This was a serious development, and Katie's face reflected her alarm.

'About you in the British army, I suppose?'

'Yea, there were two. The first one was about British soldiers, and the latest just said:

Go back to England. You are not wanted here.

'Have you any notion who might be behind this'.

'You know I wouldn't put it past Edward. He's mad jealous of me, and he was always on about going back to England'.

Katie thought that Edward was capable of anything, but this did not seem to be his way of doing things.

'No, I don't think Edward would stoop to doing that to his brother. Anyway, he's more likely just to come out and say it. I mean, he's not likely to carry a can of paint and a brush here and back home again, is he?'

Despite Katie's strong recommendation to the contrary, Robert had no intention of reporting it to the guards. The guards might do their best, but they couldn't keep the house under twenty-four-hour surveillance.

'Whoever it is will soon get tired of it. I hope for his sake I don't get my hands on him. I would ram that paintbrush of his up his arse'.

Katie was worried. She didn't like her fiancé being harassed like this, but more so, she dreaded the consequences of Robert encountering the offender as he defaced the walls. Robert was angry enough to hurt the man, or worse still, Robert could suffer serious injury himself.

Katie wondered if someone in Murphy's might remember selling blue paint.

'I thought the same thing and enquired about it. That colour is not popular at all. The only ones who bought that colour in the last while were Mrs Cosgrove and the priest's housekeeper, and they are not likely to be crossing the river at night to paint a message on my wall. No, it's probably an old pot of paint lying around for a while. I'm sure my father had that colour on rafters in a cattle shed years ago'.

Katie considered it time to lighten the atmosphere.

'Robert, come on, we'll go for a walk down the low road and get a bit of air'.

He readily agreed and stopped to lock his front door.

'Isn't it a pity that we don't have a few man traps that we could set around the place'.

'What are they, when they are at home?'

Robert told her that they were like gigantic rat traps. Seemingly, in the old days the landlords had problems with poachers coming onto their land so they began to set those traps around the place. The springs in those were strong enough to break a man's leg'.

Katie laughed. I can't see the law letting you use one of those here. Maybe, it's a woman trap you need.

He gave a nervous laugh.

'Well, I'd never have a problem with women calling to me. If she was good looking, a woman caller could paint the whole house blue and the town red for all I'd care'.

Katie smiled along, fully sure that he was trying to wind her up. Anyway, it provided her with an opening to enquire what he and Alice would chat about.

'Ah, she used to talk about the lads she met at the dances and what she thought of them. She told me about Edward moping around the back of the halls, not dancing with anyone'.

'Did she ever talk about getting back with Edward?'

'I think that relationship is dead in the water. The same Alice won't be stuck for a man. She has a lot to offer'.

Katie heard herself asking a question that might be better unasked.

'Is that right? And if I wasn't around, would you fancy your chances with her?'

Robert was uncomfortable fielding that question.

He looked at Katie, wondering how serious she was. That proved difficult to gauge. Nevertheless, he opted for a glib response.

'If she already fancied an O' Connor, she might like the brand. I could be in there', he laughed.

'And why do you think I am here?' she teased.

It was a conversation Robert would prefer not to engage in.

Katie had more to say on the matter.

'Alice Kelly blanks me now when I see her, or else gives me a pitiful look. Who does that woman think she is? It's not my fault that the two O' Connor brothers prefer me to her'.

Robert decided to let the remark pass without any further comment.

Again Katie had a different idea.

'If I wasn't around, would you have gone out with her? She is attractive. I'm sure you can see that'.

'She is attractive, but she wouldn't do much for me. I don't think we could have a future together'.

'You took time to consider that, I see, and do you mind telling me why you think that?'

Robert found himself clutching at straws in an attempt to deal with her line of questioning.

'There's no spark between Alice and me. It's different with you. Every time I pass by you, I want to grab your arse. I don't feel that way about her'.

That reply seemed to offer some comfort to Katie, but her worried look remained.

Robert felt that he needed to put her out of her misery.

'Katie', he said, fixing her in one of his earnest gazes.

'You know there isn't anything going on between Alice and me'.

'I know that, and if I thought for a moment there was, I'd gouge her eyes out and do some permanent damage elsewhere to you'.

'It's good to know that my eyes would come safe anyway'.

'It would not be your eyes that would be damaged, if you catch my drift'.

Robert understood only too well.

'I get the picture'.

Chapter 37

Katie had roped Robert into doing some work around the farm whenever he was available. Joseph could not be expected to do everything himself. Katie and her mother helped out in every way they could, but there were times when outside help was needed. Robert was glad to help out, but he soon grew very tired of it. Apart from not liking farm work, he felt that his good nature had been taken advantage of. Anyway, there was no fun attached to it. Joseph was not exactly a barrel of laughs. The lad was a bit innocent in the world's ways and only wanted to talk to Robert about military hardware. He felt that Margaret never fully trusted him, no matter what help he gave to the family. Robert greatly resented this.

Even though he must have known that he was an unwelcome caller, Edward dropped in occasionally to assist with the farm chores. On one occasion, he even brought his scythe to help with the mowing. Margaret and Joseph appreciated this, but it was a source of great annoyance to Katie. She knew it was simply an attempt to win favour with her family. After two or three such visits, and at the suggestion of Katie, Joseph asked him not to call again. Edward resented this but made no fuss about it at the time.

However, later on, his resentment found expression. The following week, he managed to waylay Katie as she emerged onto the main road from the Carrington's avenue.

'So, you don't think Joseph needs more help on the farm', he began.

Katie was angered to be thus ambushed but not surprised. On this occasion, she was determined not to be intimidated. This sort of behaviour had to stop. She steeled herself to be as strong as she needed to be.

She got down from her bike at the unoccupied gatehouse, and stood toe to toe with her stalker.

'Listen here, Edward. This following me has to stop. Let me be straight with you. I don't want you to talk to me or to help me or help any of my family. In fact, I don't want to see you at all'.

She was enraged, and even though Edward was looking more agitated by the moment, she continued to berate him.

'What sort of bloody freak are you, hanging around the roads, hiding in the ditches waiting for a woman, who does not even want to share the same county as you? Go away and get a woman who wants to be with you,' she fumed.

Edward had presumed that he would have the upper hand in the encounter as the time and the setting were of his choosing. He had his lines well rehearsed too, but he was wrong-footed by Katie's unexpected outburst. The woman was tougher than he could have imagined. He felt humiliated, but his wounded pride only served to make him more aggressive.

He took a quick look to ensure that no one was approaching from either direction, before he reached out and grabbed her around the waist. He lifted her from the road and pushed her up against the wall. Katie began to scream.

His rough right hand covered her mouth and stifled her cries.

Katie feared for her life but remained perfectly still lest she agitate him further.

'Now, you have had your say. It is my turn to talk. And what's more, you are going to listen'.

She was in no position to argue and prayed that someone else might appear on the scene.

Edward swallowed hard before he spoke.

When he began to talk, his voice took on a strange calmness.

'Right, Miss High and Mighty, if that is the way you feel about it, I want nothing to do with you either. In future, I'm not even going to look the side of the road you are on. You can stick with that selfish brother of mine if you want. Anyway, you'll soon see him for what he is. I wasted my time with you. And don't go around the place claiming I attacked you because I didn't. I just needed to be heard'.

Edward then removed his hand from her mouth, and for one awful moment, she feared that he would strike her.

He didn't.

He turned around and began to walk up the road. He had a parting shot for her.

'And don't be trying to paint me as some mad lunatic. I'm not the mad one around here,' he hissed.

Katie was too shocked to reply. Her entire body was shaking, and her legs felt like they could no longer support her.

She felt faint.

After a moment or two her breathing gradually slowed down to its normal levels.

It took her a further ten minutes before she felt capable of getting back on her bicycle.

When she did, she pedalled as fast as she could and did not look behind her until she was safely home.

Chapter 38

When Robert heard about Katie's terrifying incident, he was greatly concerned and enraged. Even in the retelling, he could see that her eyes were full of terror. Edward had to be confronted. Such behaviour could no longer be tolerated. He would also tell his parents about this. Who knows, Edward might not seem so reliable and stable after that revelation?

The heir apparent to the O'Connor lands might have shot himself in the foot.

Next day, Robert dropped in on his parents. They had not seen Edward since breakfast time, and they were very worried about him.

'The lad is losing it completely', Tommy told him.

'He has gone as wild as the wind, and all over that woman of yours. Jaysus, Robert, couldn't you give him Katie and let's be done with all of this?'

The question was not to be taken seriously and was born out of exasperation.

Julia could never understand her husband's odd sense of humour, but it helped him to ease the tension building up in him.

'If you have never been hurt, it's easy to be glib', she reflected.

Robert hoped that Edward might have moved on from his infatuation with Katie. He relayed in detail the events of the previous evening. His parents exchanged knowing looks, indicating that this was an increased level of seriousness.

From their reports, Edward had become more and more disconnected from normal life and routine. On two evenings recently, he was still in the town when he would normally have been milking the cows. Tommy had taken him to task over this, but his words did not register with Edward.

A neighbour had also experienced problems with Edward.

Mrs Gallagher had complained to Tommy that her cattle were being released onto the road. Edward denied that he had left the gate open, but his recent erratic behaviour made Tommy believe that his neighbour was telling the truth.

He also thought that this situation might cure itself.

'Robert, I think we have to cut him a bit of slack and hope he will soon see sense. There's nothing to be gained by coming the heavy with him. I imagine, it's like any other illness. It will have to take its course'.

As they were chatting, Edward calmly walked through the front door. He was surprised to see Robert there, and he clearly resented his presence.

He looked angrily at his younger brother, but said nothing.

It was Robert who was first to speak.

'You played the big bully with Katie yesterday. Do you get a kick out of frightening young women?' Robert asked.

Edward smirked at his brother's remarks.

'She would need to get used to that treatment if she intends to spend her life with you. Ex-soldiers are not supposed to make for nice husbands, well not British soldiers anyway'.

Robert was stung by the comment and rose to approach him, but Julia's intervention made him reconsider. Instead, he contented himself with a verbal warning to his brother.

'If you ever go near Katie again, you will have me to deal with'.

Edward stood up with a look of angry defiance.

Fearing violence, Tommy was on his feet, calling for peace.

'You boys should remember where you are and who you are and show respect to your home and mother. We don't want a Leitrim version of Cain and Abel here'.

Robert was forced to bite his tongue and count to ten.

Edward shouted that he was finished bothering about Katie anyway. The woman was bad news, and he wanted nothing more to do with her.

'All I feel for her now is pity that she is saddled with a thick like you'.

Robert's ten-second count was not sufficient to quell his rage.

'I'll show you who is thick', Robert shouted as he rose and crossed the kitchen floor, to confront his brother.

Tommy rushed to place his body between them. Like a referee in a boxing contest, he extended his arms to avoid injury being done.

Both men hurled punches in each other's direction. Most punches failed to land, but Edward got caught with a right hook that sent blood pumping from his nose.

The sight of spilled blood raised temperatures all-round.

Julia's hysterical shrieks made for an eerie and surreal backdrop.

'Oh, they are going to kill one another. God help us'.

She considered the one who landed the blow to be the instigator of the violence.

'Robert, get out of this house and don't come back. Any man who lifts his hand to his sick brother is not welcome here'.

Robert made his way to the door, angrily striking his knuckles on the door frame as he departed.

Despite his enraged state, he immediately knew that he had acted improperly. He regretted striking his brother. His only defence was that he had been provoked.

Chapter 39

Despite Katie's more frequent visits to the cottage, she could never leave the worries of home behind her. Robert vainly tried to distract her into enjoying their moments of privacy together, but Katie always seemed to be fretting about some problem in the Higgins household. Gerry's death made her feel much more responsible for everyone. Right now, it was her mother's anguish concerning Delia, her critically ill sister, which was uppermost in her mind.

Apparently, Auntie Delia was not long for this world. Her husband, Paddy had pleaded with Margaret to come for a final visit as Delia had been asking for her.

There was only one thing for it. Margaret would have to travel to Belfast to see her sister one last time. Margaret had to deal with the recent loss of her husband, and now her sister was seriously ill. Life can be very challenging at times.

Katie was adamant that her mother should not travel on her own, especially in her fragile state. As a dutiful daughter, she stepped up and took charge of arrangements. She would travel with her mother and provide her with the support and companionship she would need.

First of all, she had to clear it with her employers. The Carringtons had no problem with her taking some leave.

Unfortunately, she had not informed Robert of her plans.

When he eventually learned that she would be away for a week, he was far from impressed. The man had only got used to having her back in his life after the bereavement. Now she was going to be absent again. Not only that, but he had been asked to look in on Joseph while the two women were away.

Robert voiced no complaint, but his glum expression told its own story.

Katie was disappointed with his attitude and had no qualms about telling him so.

'I couldn't allow my grieving mother to travel on trains and buses on her own like you might send a package, and she agitated about her dead husband and dying sister'.

Robert knew that he was in a no-win situation.

'It's fine! If you have to go, you have to go. It's as simple as that'.

'So why the long face?'

'I don't have a long face. I'm just trying to figure how you can take a notion of going somewhere, and you just up and go. But when I want to go somewhere, I have to clear it with you first and you might block the whole thing'.

In Katie's mind, Robert was displaying all the symptoms of a serious bout of the sulks.

She wondered how he could equate her visiting a sick aunt in the North with his moving to London for the year. To Robert, however, it was the same principle.

'I consulted with you in advance, but you only mentioned it to me because you wanted me to look after Joseph for you'.

Katie was indignant.

'Well, I never! Robert O' Connor, you are showing yourself to be mean-spirited and selfish. You are no longer the kind character I fell in love with. You have become selfish. When did you last think of anybody but yourself?'

Robert just threw his hands in the air from frustration and sullenly made his exit.

Katie accepted that she should have acquainted him of her plans earlier. That would have avoided much of the bad feeling on the matter.

She had not emerged well from this situation. She regretted upsetting him especially as she would not see him again for another week. While he was still in earshot, she shouted after him

'I'm sorry, Robert. I still love you. I really do. See you next Sunday night.'

Chapter 40

Absence makes the heart grow fonder, and on Sunday night, Robert was delighted to see Katie back at his door. He rose to greet her. The bad feeling from their last meeting had been consigned to the past.

'I wanted to collect you at the station, but I knew Joseph would collect your mother, and you would probably want to see her safely home first'.

Katie accepted the wisdom of this call.

'Yea, this is a better arrangement. Come on, give me a big hug. I certainly could do with one'.

Robert held her in his arms and gripped her tightly. It felt good. She had almost forgotten how safe and secure she felt when lovingly enveloped in his arms.

'How's the Aunt?' he asked.

Katie stepped back from the embrace before answering him.

'She's still hanging in there. It was great for Mother to visit her. I think it helped to get her mind off things at home for a while. You have no idea how much she misses my father'.

There was just a hint of a tear forming in her eye as she spoke. To retain her composure she sought some distraction in a change of subject.

'Joseph said you were a great help in moving the cattle. Thank you for your help, and I want you to know that I really appreciate it'.

'No problem! I dropped over whenever I could'.

'Thank you so much'.

'I think you should go away more often', Robert smiled delighted at the attention he was receiving.

'We should make up more', she ventured, throwing off her coat and placing it on the back of the nearest chair.

They talked for ages about events in the village, on the farm and the days spent in Belfast.

She had stories to tell about cross-border inspections.

'The custom officers came onto the train, looking for any smuggled stuff'.

Robert expected as much.

'People say that along the border, there is great money to be made from smuggling'.

He pretended that he was interested in getting involved in that business.

'Jaysus! That might be an idea for a man to make a few extra bob'.

Even though he was only winding her up, Katie rose to the bait.

'What on earth could you smuggle? Anyway, knowing our luck at times, you'd probably be caught and have to serve time in a pokey wee cell'.

Robert felt that she was being over-dramatic.

'I don't think you get jail for small-time smuggling. You'd probably get a stiff fine'.

'And where would we get money to pay your fine?

No, Robert, you can put that thought right out of your mind'.

'Katie, I was only winding you up'.

That statement seemed to put an end to the discussion on contraband.

'How's Alice? ' Katie asked out of the blue.

'She hasn't visited since you left, if that is what you were wondering, but I see her in Murphy's'.

'Any man on the horizon?'

'No, there's always something wrong with every bloke she meets'.

'I suppose you have to be over one man completely before taking up with another', Katie said.

'Do you reckon?'

'I do, and by the way, is there any news from your family since I left?'

'Well, I was talking to my mother. She dropped into the yard to see me about Norah's wedding. She wants no bad atmosphere in front of the Martins, so we'll all keep up a civilised front'.

Katie had been looking forward to the wedding, but her recent bereavement had put paid to that and even pushed her own wedding date into 1947. She hoped Robert could report on the style and gossip, but men are hopeless in that regard. If Alice was still going with Edward, she could have heard all from her, but circumstances put paid to that also.

Chapter 41

The wedding of Hughie Martin and Norah O'Connor took place in warm September sunshine in the village church. The church ceremony was at half-past eight in the morning. There was a relatively small congregation there, composed mainly of family members and an assortment of friends and relations.

After the church ceremony, the bridal party travelled to Sligo town via the Lower Road for the wedding breakfast. After the meal, the traditional speeches were delivered. All contributions were greeted with polite applause and a sprinkling of laughter in the appropriate places. It was a very civilised event.

The bridegroom was positively beaming. He proclaimed himself to be the happiest man in the entire country. He had married a good woman from a decent family. He was confident that they would be very happy together, and expressed his appreciation to the O' Connor family for entrusting their beautiful daughter into his care.

Tommy O' Connor and his wife Julia were delighted that their daughter was suitably married. It was the only high point of their year thus far. There was much to recommend their new son-in-law. Hubert Martin came from a respectable family who farmed a considerable holding. The fact that he was of a gentle and kind disposition as well as a practising Catholic meant that he was an excellent match for Norah. Her father spoke of the pleasure he took in welcoming Hughie into the family.

The only shadow over the event for the O' Connors was their son's recent rather eccentric behaviour. Edward had sat on his own in the church, refusing to share a pew with his brother Robert. Julia had been worried about his troubled state over recent weeks. She had determined that they would keep a close eye on him during the day. On several occasions during the day, Robert attempted to make his peace with Edward, but to no avail. Offers of drink were refused, and attempts at random small talk were met with silent scorn. However, Edward was not offensive and went out of his way to tell his new brother-in-law that he was pleased that they were now related.

The groom expressed the hope that Edward would soon find happiness in his own relationships.

'Edward, you will find a good woman too, and we could all be back here in a few years, only this time celebrating your marriage'.

'Thanks, Hughie, it's all in hand'.

'Good man, Edward, do you have your eyes set on any particular girl?'

'There's only one for me, but I have messed up there'.

'Well, maybe you need a break from women. There's plenty more fish in the sea, as the man says'.

'True, Hughie, but I'm not interested in fish'.

Later that night, the O' Connors arrived back at the family homestead without their daughter, Norah. The house seemed eerily empty without her. She and her new husband were starting their honeymoon in Salthill, a favourite resort of the Martin family.

Back home and relaxing in their fireside chairs, Tommy and Julia began to consider the events of the day. There was much to be pleased with. Julia, in particular, was delighted that the family had not let her down. She knew that she would miss Norah terribly, but she was glad that her daughter had married well.

Edward sat down on the opposite side of the kitchen table, just staring into vacancy or so it seemed. Very soon, it appeared that his stare was fixed on something in the mid-distance. Suddenly, and without any warning, he started to bang his head off the wooden table in a slow rhythmic fashion. Tommy raced over and attempted to hold his head up.

'Jaysus Edward, I don't know what you were on today, but you can't go beating your head off the kitchen table'.

Edward stopped banging his head but became more agitated than before. His arms began to flail widely, and he became incoherent.

'They are trying to do me down, but I will not let them. Look at them! They think I don't see them, but they are hiding over there. I know who sent them', he roared.

'What are you on about,' Julia enquired.

'Who do you see, Edward?'

Edward looked at her with a cold stare in his dark brown eyes.

'You can never see them. They are not after you'.

Julia was getting more worried by the minute.

There was no indication of intoxication on Edward's part. Nobody there had seen him drinking during the wedding. Tommy, fearing for the worst suggested sending for the doctor.

'The poor lad maybe needs an injection or some other type of treatment to settle him'.

Julia needed convincing. She viewed the episode as a shameful event. With a bit of luck, it might have passed before morning.

'It would be great if things got better of their own accord.'

It was only when Edward began to strip off in the kitchen that Julia relented and agreed to send for the doctor.

By the time the doctor arrived, Edward had settled somewhat and was sitting cross-legged on the settle bed, wrapped in the quilt with his eyes staring straight ahead of him. He did not seem to be totally aware of his surroundings.

As before, the doctor was the epitome of calm.

'Edward, I hear you are under a bit of pressure. I will check your pulse and have a look at the old blood pressure'.

Edward looked at him. He offered no resistance but did not interact with him in any way.

Dr Clarke finished his examination and moved across the room to where the anguished parents sat forlorn and confused. It had been one crazy day. A few short hours earlier, they celebrated their daughter's wedding, and now they were coping with what they would have seen as the greatest affliction to befall any family.

The doctor looked across at Edward as he chatted with his parents. 'I see what you mean. He is very agitated and distressed. He might look settled now, but his pulse is still racing'.

'Can you give him something?' Tommy queried.

'I will give him a sedative, but that will wear off in a few hours. We need longer term care for Edward'.

'A good night's sleep might do him a power of good', Julia said,
clutching at straws for some hope of a miraculous recovery.

Doctor Clarke nodded, but was far from convinced.

'You know, Mrs O' Connor, your son's mind is troubled over
something, and I would guess that this has been festering for a long
time. That issue will have to be confronted. It's a bit like when a
splinter gets under your skin and into your finger. You can't reach it,
so you leave it there hoping for the best.

But, it will always fester and come to the surface. The mind is
something like that finger, and if we could find out what was
bothering him, we could start working on that. Otherwise, the
problem could go from bad to worse'.

Tommy and Julia exchanged worried looks before inviting the
doctor to sit down.

Julia, ever eager to help her son, acquainted the medic with Edward's
recent history.

'It all makes sense now. Well, now that we know that, we have
somewhere to start'.

'Do you think you can cure him of that, Doctor?' Tommy asked,
more out of hope than expectation.

'Well, I think you know what has to happen next'.

'You mean, the mental, don't you', Tommy asked.

This was their worst nightmare playing out in front of them.

Julia blessed herself and uttered a prayer to St. Jude for strength in
this seemingly hopeless case facing her.

'Yea, I know what you are thinking, but if he receives the proper treatment, he will be back home with you soon and be back to his normal, healthy self again. Stress and anguish can unhinge any of us'.

'So, Doctor, he's not mad, is he?' Tommy wondered.

'No, he's just a young man who cracked under pressure, and the quicker the experts get working on him, the better'.

The Doctor's advice was to get Edward to the hospital as soon as possible. He even volunteered to drive Edward there.

'I think there is a danger of his getting so upset that he might harm himself or someone else'.

Nobody wanted that on their conscience, so Julia and Tommy made the trip into Sligo for the second time that day. They followed the same route in the doctor's car as they followed that morning on their way to their daughter's wedding breakfast. The mood was much darker now, and the darkness over the still waters of Lough Gill reflected the shadows over their previously happy lives.

On the outskirts of Sligo Town, they took a right turn into the Short Walk and over Mental Hospital Road. The grey, imposing building of St. Columba's Mental Hospital stood ready to receive Edward. Its bright lights seemed to offer hope of brighter days ahead.

Dr Clarke asked them to wait in the car while he helped process his admission.

In a few minutes, he returned alone.

'They are ready for Edward now. They have a nice bed waiting, and they will begin assessing him in the morning.'

Julia and the Doctor accompanied Edward through the front entrance before handing him over to the care of the professionals.

Chapter 42

Robert was at work when he heard of his brother's hospitalisation. He immediately went into Murphy's kitchen to share the news with Alice Kelly. She cried as he told her what he had heard. Edward and she may have gone their separate ways, but there were still tender feelings on her part.

'Poor Edward, he must have been suffering something awful'.

Robert was surprised too. He had no idea that his brother was so close to the brink. When they had quarrelled, he did not realise that his brother was mentally unwell. Robert feared he would be painted as a bigger bastard than ever because he had raised his fist to his mentally ill brother.

'Do they allow visitors in there?' Alice wondered.

'They allow visitors, but the senior man there advised against anyone visiting him for the first week anyway. They want to figure out what they are dealing with'.

'Poor Edward', Alice repeated.

'We should have suspected something like this'.

Robert felt that everyone is wise in hindsight, but how could he have suspected anything like this? He feared that his family would blame him for the whole sorry mess.

Katie only became aware of Edward's fate later that evening. Naturally, she was shocked, and soon began to examine her role in the sorry business.

'I should not have given out to him. It only maddened him. I think I might have pushed him over the edge', she cried.

'You pushed him nowhere. What encouragement did you ever give him?'

'None!'

'Well, there you are then'.

During the day, not one customer mentioned Edward to Robert, but they were all familiar with the situation. They spoke about it in hushed tones when Robert was well out of earshot. It made for fascinating gossip, but it was not something any of them would have wished on their worst enemies. Robert took some risks in visiting his home place the following evening. It was something that he felt he should do regardless of the reception he might receive.

On entering, he observed his father and mother sitting on opposite sides of the fireplace in their respective fireside chairs. They looked a sad and lonely pair, with not a word being spoken between them. A quick look at his mother's lips informed Robert that she was silently praying for her troubled son.

'So, it's you', his father said in greeting.

'Can I come in?'

'Come in. You might as well. The damage is done now'.

'I never meant to…I never knew'.

Tommy was not in his usual forgiving mood.

'You never think. That's the trouble with you, Robert, and you always do what you feel like doing without considering others'.

Julia quickly sprung to her feet lest another family dispute begin.

'God Almighty, put an end to all this bickering. We should be offering prayers for Edward's return to good health, not fighting each other about who is to blame. We can't say for certain whether any of us is to blame or none of us is to blame'.

'You are right, Love', Tommy said, rising to take his rosary beads from on top of the mantelpiece.

'Let the three of us kneel and say the three sorrowful mysteries for Edward's full recovery'.

'In the name of the Holy Spirit, thou oh Lord, may open my lips…

The Rosary was recited. Whatever it may have done for Edward, it helped improve the atmosphere in the house.

'I went into the post office today to ring the hospital. Thank God the doctor holds out good hope for him', Julia reported.

Tommy accepted that Edward had not been right for ages.

'I noticed that he used to get very cranky when people asked him about getting married. I know he was awful fond of Katie, but after you arrived back, it became an obsession'.

Robert agreed that his own return marked a defining moment in the whole business.

Julia was not bothered with any sort of analysis of cause and effect. She was concerned only with Edward getting better.

'I gave the priest money for two Masses, and he said he will say a Holy Office for him too. And I'm praying every minute of the waking day and most of the night too. God give me strength'.

Julia boiled up the kettle, and all three sat over to the table for a mug of tea and some slices of brown bread.

'Sorry it's not the freshest, but I couldn't bake today. My heart wasn't in it'.

Robert asked whether Norah had been informed.

'No, let her enjoy her honeymoon. She will hear soon enough, and hopefully, things will have improved by then'.

After a week, Edward was adjudged to be slowly responding to treatment. The doctors had been working to settle on a particular treatment that worked best on him. The doctor was encouraging in his assessment.

'Your son wants to get better. I can see that, and I am very encouraged, Mrs O' Connor'.

Julia blessed herself at that positive assessment.

Robert considered visiting his brother in the hospital but decided against it.

He would wait until Edward was better able for it.

Chapter 43

Julia and Tommy made the return trip on three occasions every week to visit their son. They initially feared the worst-case scenario, that their son might be permanently institutionalised. They were quickly assured that this would not be the case. However, there was no predicting the time frame involved. Every case was unique, but Edward was likely to be hospitalised for several months.

Each time they visited, they did so with a heavy heart. Julia cried on the train journey to Sligo and also on the return trip. Once in her son's presence, she had to steel herself to be strong for him. She and Tommy never spoke of Edward during the long walk from Sligo railway station to St. Columba's, as Julia did not want her eyes to be red from crying. They were determined to keep the bright side out for their son.

Until his mother mentioned it, Robert was unaware that Alice had already visited his brother in the hospital. Alice had been pleasantly surprised to find Edward, dressed smartly, sitting up in a chair. She had been half expecting to see him alone in the corner of a large dayroom.

The everyday nature of his surroundings had been a further pleasant surprise for her. Edward, she reported, was subdued and looked sedated, but he seemed at peace. He even smiled as she entered the room.

She intended to visit him again, but she did not feel comfortable talking about Edward anymore. This was a disappointment for Robert who was keen to know when her next visit might be.

She resented his questioning and went on the attack.

'Have I to run everything past you?' she snapped

'No, but I thought we were close enough that you might mention it.
He is my brother after all'.

'Don't you think I know that?'

She was tempted to lash out, but hesitated lest she say something she
might later regret. Despite her anger, she struggled to retain
composure. Her words, when they came, were slow and measured,
even though her voice was shaking.

'Robert, let's get this straight. We are not friends and never will be
friends. You used me, and I used you. That is all there is to it'.

Robert was taken aback by her hostile attitude towards him.

'It was only a few weeks ago when we got up very close and
personal'.

Alice dropped her head at the recollection and emitted a low,
plaintive cry.

'I don't need any reminding of that'.

'What's up, Alice? Is there something troubling you?'

She stifled her tears before looking him straight in the eye.

'If you must know, I have had no period since we got up close and
personal, as you put it'.

When the impact of her words registered, Robert's heart seemed to
stop for one perceptible moment.

Even though he had readily understood, he asked her what exactly
she meant.

'For God's sake, do I have to draw pictures for you?' she asked,
attempting to stem the flow of tears from her two sad eyes.

Robert attempted to assimilate what he had just heard.

'And are you normally regular in that sort of thing'?

'I'm as regular as clockwork in that sort of thing, and that's why I'm worried, Robert. I am really and truly worried. I am worried to death that I could be pregnant'.

Robert had never considered such a possibility.

'Jaysus, that's a big worry. What are you going to do? Are you going to the doctor or what?'

'No, I'm not going to any doctor. But, I'll tell you one thing for nothing. If I am pregnant with your child, you will marry me and at damn short notice too. Given a choice, I would prefer to marry your brother, confused and all as he might be now, but that is not on. There is only one thing for it. If I am pregnant, you will have to face up to your responsibilities'.

Robert was rocked by that possibility. It was almost too much for his mind to take in.

He was so shaken that he barely noticed her leaving his company. Some hours later, Robert did what he always did when he was beset by problems. He sought refuge in alcohol. He needed to escape from this pitiful situation. The bar of the Abbey Hotel was a good place to start. There were few people in the bar except a few men from up the mountain, whom he knew only by sight. Robert sat down in a quiet corner alone with his thoughts.

Before he was altogether incoherent, his old neighbour, Josie Taylor, joined him.

'Drinking on your own, Robert, that's a bad sign', Josie said by way of greeting.

'And I suppose you just called in to see the time on the big clock here,' Robert responded.

Robert ordered the drinks, and the two men fell into conversation.

'Is it woman trouble, Robert, or is Murphy being awkward with you?'

Robert could only admire the older man's powers of perception.

'The lead-up to a wedding can be trying on a woman's nerves', he conceded.

Josie did not take the answer at face value, and speculated that the business with Edward and Alice might also be playing on his mind.

'I hear Edward had a thing for your woman'.

It was embarrassing to talk about. Anyone else might have been told to go away and mind his own business, but not Josie.

'He certainly had a thing for Katie, and it has upset the whole, bloody applecart. Edward is in the asylum. Alice is giving out, and Katie is upset. At times I wish that I could walk away from it all. A man does not expect that from a brother'.

'Yea, Robert, but some women get more admirers than others'.

There was no arguing that point.

Several drinks later and Robert was becoming more boisterous. The barman indicated to Josie that it might be time to get Robert out of there.

Robert had no intention of leaving. His increasingly inebriated state helped loosen his tongue and remove some inhibitions.

'My friend in London is onto me about a job there. I can tell you there are times when I consider walking out on Murphy, on the parents, on silly bloody Edward and all the women and start a new life in London'.

Josie knew that Robert was feeling particularly low.

He tried to keep the conversation relaxed and uncontroversial.

'I know it's tempting, but for a start, I'm sure you'd miss Katie Higgins'.

Josie felt obliged to stay with Robert and escort him safely home. In the time they spent together, he had only consumed one drink for every three by the younger man. When closing time came around, the barman was only too glad to see the back of Robert.

It was a calm but cool night as Josie linked his drunken friend down the walkway behind the hotel, over the little bridge, along the tree-lined walk before finishing at the humble cottage on the edge of the cemetery.

Josie saw Robert safely into the cottage. He tried to get him to bed, but Robert stubbornly resisted his efforts, preferring to collapse into a bedside chair.

'I'm not going into bed. I'm going to stay awake the whole bloody night. I can't take another night of those awful nightmares'.

'What nightmares are these? Don't tell me that the ghosts are coming in the door to you'.

'No ghosts, just the memory of the terrible things from the war'.

Josie strove to be positive and optimistic.

'Well, it's not real. You know that when you wake in the morning, you will be in your own bed, safe and sound and the war all over'.

That was of little consolation to Robert.

'It's real to me. The war is never over while it still rages in your head', he replied, wagging his right hand's index finger to emphasise the point.

'What sort of things are we talking about?'

'Every sort of terrible things!'

'You mean killing the Germans?'

Robert sat up straight in the chair and became animated.

It almost seemed as if he had sobered up in record time.

'That's the funny thing. I could never say for sure that I killed anyone. I certainly shot at them, and I hit some, but I couldn't say whether they were dead or just wounded for the life of me. My problem was not the Germans. It was watching your pals die, watching the bloke you shared your billet with, die a slow and painful death, listening to the shrieks and the screams and the mad shouting and cursing. It would nearly make you want to turn your gun on yourself".

Josie thought that, for a man who had been very drunk, Robert was being remarkably lucid about his nightly visitations. He suggested that the doctor might be able to prescribe some medicine that might ease matters for him.

'There will be no drugs, Josie. I don't want to end up a drugged-up dope. I would rather be piss drunk than a bloody vegetable'.

'Do you get these nightmares every night?'

'Nights that I'm wrecked tired or drunk are my best nights. If you kick open that locker there, you'll see my own sleeping medication'.

Josie did what he was told and lifted out a naggin bottle of *Paddy* whiskey.

'*Paddy* and I get on well. I would be stuck without him but he's not as good as he was. I have to drink more and more of him to have any effect on me at all. Isn't it a terrible day that a man can't get drunk on neat whiskey when he bloody well needs to'.

Josie encouraged Robert to hit the sack anyway and hope for the best.

'You better set the alarm clock for work in the morning because I think you'll be dead to the world by opening time'.

'I don't own a bloody alarm clock. And I don't need one. I am always awake for hours before I need to be up. I will be at work on time'.

Chapter 44

Despite his predictions to the contrary, Robert was late for work in the morning. It wasn't because he had slept in. It was more a case of his not sleeping at all. Alice's news had given him much to think about that he lost track of time. It was nearly eleven o'clock before he appeared in his workplace. Mr Murphy was not impressed.

'You are late, Mr O' Connor and I hope you have a very good reason for that'.

'I have, Mr Murphy. I was sick as a dog last night.'

'I am sure you were, but I am equally sure that your sickness was self-inflicted. The stench of alcohol from you would make a horse weak at the knees. You are not in any fit condition to perform your duties today'.

Robert feared that he might be given his walking papers there and then, but Joseph Murphy was a more considerate employer than perhaps Robert deserved.

'Go home and sleep it off, and if you ever present yourself in this state again, you will not only be out of a job but out of accommodation as well'.

Robert had little choice but to turn on his heel and return home.

On his way out of the yard, Robert encountered Alice Kelly crossing the road from the meat stall.

'So, you finally decided to show your face, did you?'

'The boss sent me home. It seems I'm not fit to serve his precious customers!'

Alice was not surprised.

'You can't blame him. You smell like a bloody brewery. You are lucky that he didn't give you your cards'.

'He happened to mention that too'.

Alice looked around before moving her head closer to his.

'Well you should keep Mr Murphy happy because you might be taking on extra responsibilities soon and I don't mean your previous understanding with Katie'.

Robert was left standing alone with his thoughts as Alice slipped in the side door to the kitchen. While trudging back to the cottage, Robert resisted a strong temptation to return to the hotel bar for a hair of the dog that bit him.

Back at base, he stripped off and slipped back under the blankets. He needed to catch up on some sleep, but his mind was racing with all sorts of frightening possibilities, that threatened his future. He made a supreme effort to clear his mind, and by one o' clock he was dead to the world. He was still dead to the world when Katie came hammering on his door at seven o'clock that evening.

Robert struggled to the door and opened it.

Katie looked both surprised and worried.

'I met Alice, and she told me that you were sick and had to go home early.

Robert wrongly presumed that Alice had depicted him in a bad light. 'When did you see Alice?'

'I met her on the street a few minutes ago. She told me that you had been feeling poorly and had to go home'.

She seemed genuinely sorry to hear that he was ill, but the stench of stale alcohol on his breath told its own story.

Her mood quickly changed.

'Robert O' Connor, I never thought you would be stupid enough to drink on a work night'.

'I suppose I had a few too many'.

That was already obvious to her.

She wondered who the bad influence might be.

The questions were coming thick and fast.

'I was drinking on my own. Josie Taylor joined me for a while. He must have thought that I needed company'.

Katie could not believe that he could be so stupid as to risk everything for a few moments of pleasure.

'Did you not think that you could lose your job and the roof over your head that went with the job?

'I seem to be the only one who didn't think that. But the thing is that he didn't throw me out'.

'That's no thanks to you. You have to learn to be mature and responsible. You can't be doing what you want all the time. You have to be think beyond the moment', she stressed.

Robert was annoyed that people seemed to be taking it on themselves to lecture him about life and responsibility.

Katie continued to look him in the eye as if desperately attempting to find some explanation for his foolish behaviour.

'What, in hell, possessed you to go drinking last night in the first place?'

Robert could not confess the reason behind this drinking binge. He hoped she would never be any wiser about that.

He was in a corner and was desperate to put an end to her questioning. He decided to play the sympathy card.

'Listen, Katie, the nightmares have been worse than ever the last few nights. I was nearly afraid of going to bed, so I thought maybe having a few scoops might help dull my brain a bit'.

Katie fell for the explanation. She immediately got to her feet and threw her arms around him.

'Robert, I'm so sorry for giving out to you. You poor thing, coping with all that awful war stuff on your own! But when we are married, I will be there to help you'.

'I don't know about that, but I will be glad to have you in my bed for a whole load of reasons'.

Katie knew that she was being played.

'Well, Robert O' Connor, does your mind always come around to sex, no matter what we talk about? I swear to you that if I was on my death bed and drawing my last breath, you would be likely to jump my bones one last time'.

Robert's smile seemed to confirm her suspicion.

'Ideally, you should have someone else lined up for me before you passed away'.

Katie spoke about February, and how much she was looking forward to her wedding. The calendar had informed her that she was to be married on the feast day of Saint Valentine, the patron saint of lovers. She considered this to be most appropriate.

'It's a pity poor Daddy won't be there to give me away. Joseph will have to take his place. I think I would be the happiest bride ever on her wedding day if only my father were alive'.

Robert could see the tears forming in her eyes and moved to comfort her.

'Yea, he was a good man. You must miss him a sight'.

'There's not a day when I don't shed a tear for him. There is always something that I feel I have to tell him or ask him, and then I realise that he is not there and won't ever be there for me. Life can bring great joy, but it can also bring such sorrow, Robert'.

Robert nodded his agreement with this statement but felt the time was ripe for a change in the direction of the conversation.

'Jaysus, Katie, we should talk about less depressing things than nightmares and sudden death'.

Katie wiped her eye dry and attempted to lift herself out of her mournful state.

'You are so right. We should think of the great future we have. This time next year, we will be living here together as man and wife with a fire in the grate and the evening closing in on us. You must be looking forward to that too, Robert?'

'More than you could imagine, Katie'.

'How is Edward? What is the latest on him? '

'I thought we were going to talk about something more lively,' he wondered.

'So, we were, but how is he anyway?'

'I haven't heard for a couple of days now, but I intend to call to the house tomorrow evening. I'm not the most welcome there, but I want to find out what shape Edward is in'.

'Alice told me that he wasn't great when she last visited him', Katie volunteered.

'And the funny thing is Alice does not look great either. I thought she looked pale and sickly.

She told me that she had an upset stomach. Not that I should have bothered asking was she good or not, for that girl is still very off with me, as if it was my fault that Edward was into me'.

'Anyway, can I escort you back for part of the way?'

'You stay where you are and get yourself sorted out. I will be the finest.'

Chapter 45

Julia O' Connor saw Robert before he reached the front door. She was pouring a pot of tea for her husband Tommy and herself.

'You must have been born at tea time', she said by way of greeting.

The woman looked gaunt and haggard. The stress of Edward's illness was telling on her.

'You should know', Robert ventured by way of reply.

He greeted his father before easing himself down in a fireside chair, pleased at the good reception he had received.

'Were you working in the yard today? Tommy asked.

'I was there but I had little to do. It was very quiet'.

'I hear we are in line for a week or more of hard frost', Tommy informed him.

'Yea, I heard a mention of that'.

Tommy wondered what direction the wind might be blowing from on Thursday night.

'The old people used to say that whatever direction the wind is blowing from on Halloween Night is the way it will be blowing for most of the winter'.

Robert laughed as he spoke.

'Josie Taylor claims that it's Old Halloween you have to watch for. He reckons Halloween was celebrated a week later than in the olden days'.

'Trust Josie to have a different take on things', his father remarked

Julia poured tea for Robert and buttered a slice of homemade soda bread.

'We can't have you sitting there looking at us eating and not even ask if you had a mouth on you'.

Robert graciously accepted the hospitality he was offered.

'Were you talking to Alice today?' Julia enquired.

'I saw her a few times, but I wasn't chatting to her'.

'She's going in to see Edward tonight', Julia informed him.

This was news to Robert.

'It's good to see that she still is interested in him after the pain he caused her', Tommy remarked.

Robert maintained a diplomatic silence on that point, but enquired how his brother was.

His mother seemed upbeat on the matter.

'Well, they tell us he's improving. The latest treatment seems to agree with him, but he is very dopey yet. It's hard to see him getting out any day soon, and do you know what? I don't want them letting him out until he's good and ready'.

Robert nodded his appreciation of her position as his mother continued.

'At the start, I was ashamed about Edward being in the Mental Hospital, and now I don't care what anyone thinks. He's my boy, and if it takes another eight weeks or a hundred and eight weeks, that's fine as long as he's being cared for and improving, and thank God he is'.

Robert took a risk in asking about something that had been exercising his mind for some time.

'Does Edward ever mention me?'

The answer was slow in coming, but when it came, it held no great surprise for Robert.

'Not so as you would notice'.

'Does he mention Alice much?'

'Yes, he asked about her. He was happy to hear that she was coming in again'.   Julia had questions to ask Robert too. She wanted to know how Katie was bearing up and if any progress was being made on the wedding arrangements.

'Ah yea, she tells me she misses her father a lot, but things are in hand for the wedding in February'.

'You are getting one hell of a fine girl there, Robert, and I hope you know that.'

'I do surely, but getting back to Edward, how do you think he would take it if I were to show up some day at visiting time?

They had never envisaged that Robert would visit his brother in the hospital, considering that he was the main reason Edward was there in the first place.

Tommy and Julia looked at each other for inspiration.

Julia feared that it might hinder Edward's recovery, but her husband was more open to the suggestion.

'Maybe, Robert should visit him. You know Edward won't be any better until he learns to deal with all that business'.

Julia wasn't convinced, but she did not reject the notion either.

Robert viewed this as tacit approval from both parents. He intended to travel to Sligo on the following evening and call into St. Columba's.

The business of his visit had now been transacted, but Robert stayed to make a few polite enquiries as to how Norah was getting on. She was doing just fine as was her new husband.

With that information gleaned from them, Robert excused himself and returned to his accommodation.

Chapter 46

It was Halloween Night and only two days away from All Souls'
Day. Margaret Higgins was studying her List of the Dead for
November prayers. This was a list of one's relatives, which would be
submitted to the priest for special prayers during November.

Margaret had been teary during the day. It was the first occasion she
had to include her late husband's name on that list. She missed Gerry
every minute of every day. The farm kept her busy and her son
Joseph was a great help but it was Katie she relied upon.

Now Katie was on her way out too. It was a tough old world for the
widow woman. She tried her best to look joyous as Katie grew more
excited, now that winter had taken hold and the wedding day neared.
Margaret smiled, but privately wished that February would never
make its appearance. She had not the heart to tell Katie that she did
not trust her fiancé. Even though she might dismiss most young men
as being unworthy of her daughter, there was something about
Robert O' Connor that worried her.

'I thought you were meeting your fella tonight?'

'I was, but he's going to visit the brother'.

Margaret could not contain her surprise.

'He is going into the mad house on Halloween Night. That is brave
of him. At least, there's no full moon until the ninth of the month'.

'Mother, that is not a nice way to put it. Edward is sick. He's not
mad'.

'You weren't saying that a few weeks back. You know well he's
mad in the head for you. I don't know what it is with you and those
O'Connor boys'.

'It is only Robert I am in a relationship with'.

Mrs Higgins made a supreme effort not to ridicule her daughter's choice in men.

'Love, that word gets bandied about nowadays, and for the life of me I don't know what it means'

'Come on Mother, you know. You loved Daddy and he loved you. You know what love is'.

'Yea, love is about staying together for the daily struggle through hard times'.

'Surely Mother, you must have had a certain feeling that you could not explain when you met Dad. You must have found yourself smiling as you thought of him'.

Mention of her late husband made her very emotional. She dried her hands with the tea towel and sat down at the head of the kitchen table.

'Your father was a good man who always stood by my side through the good times and bad. We loved each other but there was none of that soppy stuff with us. We just got on with life'.

Katie, as much for distraction as anything else, boiled up the kettle to make a cup of tea for both of them.

'You know Mother, that Robert is going through a bad time with the horrors of war keeping him awake at night. He's drinking a bit too much at times, and he finds it hard to get sleep at all'.

Her mother appeared a bit taken aback by this revelation.

'Alcohol never solved any problem', she reckoned.

'The man who thinks that drink will sort his problems is a foolish man'.

Katie was more than a little angered by her mother's dismissive comment. She rightly interpreted it as an indictment of her fiancé. 'Are you saying Robert is not smart. He is one of the most intelligent people I ever met'.

Her mother threw her hands into the air in a disparaging manner. 'Come on, Katie! You have very limited experience of men. Some of the fellows around here wouldn't know their arse from their elbow'.

'Mother, what's needling you today? You haven't a good word to say about anyone. I don't know why I bother telling you things at all, since you turn it all back on me', she sobbed.

Margaret took a deep intake of breath and collected her thoughts. 'You are right. Since Gerry died, I have become very unhappy and bitter. I know there are great men around here. I want the best for you and sometimes I worry about your judgement. What do you expect when you tell me your man is drinking too much and he can't sleep at night because his mind is unhinged with awful memories?' And if that was not enough, his brother is locked up in the Mental Hospital. Surely that is cause enough to worry?'

Katie still felt that her mother was being needlessly dramatic, even if she was acting out of her best interests. She decided it was better to park this conversation and talk about something less controversial. 'I hear there's heavy frost on the way'.

'Yea, Joseph mentioned that. We could do without that, but hopefully it will kill some of the germs that are going around. Every second person is sneezing or sniffling. It was a bloody chorus of coughing at last Mass on Sunday. I was nearly expecting the priest to turn around and tell someone to leave the church'.

After a few moments, Joseph arrived into the kitchen.

'Well Katie, I suppose this is all wedding talk. Have you the outfit bought yet?'

'I haven't, but I would need to get something organised soon. Mother, I hope you will come shopping with me. You know I like to get your opinion on things'.

'You do, but only when it suits you', her mother laughed.

Joseph was also in the market for a wardrobe upgrade.

'I'll need a suit too, seeing that I will be giving you away. I was thinking that a navy or a slate coloured one that would be serviceable'.

'Of course you will get a suit', his mother responded. 'A half-decent suit would last you years, the odd few times you put on a collar and tie. It might even do for your own wedding'.

Joseph saw this as a welcome boost to his rather poor self-image. As yet, he had no girl friend and no sign of one on the horizon. The cursed birthmark still affected his confidence with girls, but thankfully he was now able to grow hair that masked some of it.

'Where's the groom-to-be tonight?' Joseph asked.

'He's visiting the brother', Katie answered, hoping that this was not going to spark another contentious discussion.

'Right then', Joseph continued. 'I see you two didn't wait for me before you wet the tea', he remarked as he busied himself rubbing a mug clean with the front of his shirt.

'Anyone for another drop?' he queried.

'No, work away there yourself', Katie replied.

Chapter 47

Robert wondered what might happen when he finally got to meet Edward again.

After her recent visit, Alice had reported that she had found Edward to be in fair form, but only a shadow of his former self. She realised that even if Edward were released that week, there was precious little chance that he would be a candidate for a walk down the aisle with a carnation in his label. This was all bad news for Robert.

It had always been a long shot that Edward would be champing at the bit to get back with Alice. None of this would have been of any concern to Robert had it not been for Alice's predicament. He had been hoping against hope that the girl might have been worked up over a false alarm, but that proved not to be the case.

She was now suffering from morning sickness and her situation was becoming increasingly urgent. Time was not on her side. She would begin to show soon, so she needed to have a plan.

Alice was clear in her mind about the sequencing of events.

'Robert, you should consider letting down Katie as gently as possible, and the sooner the better. You can't have a girl planning her wedding for February, and you set to marry another one in a few weeks time'.

The callous nature of the remark stunned him.

Everything had now been put into a frighteningly stark context for him. Matters could no longer be allowed to drift.

'Getting married to a man just because you are carrying his child is a poor reason to be wed', he chanced.

'Oh, and what alternative would his lordship and sire suggest?'

Robert was desperately clutching at straws.

'You could go into one of those places the nuns run, and get the baby adopted. You would be able to take over where you left off then'.

'Would I now? And this would suit you nicely, wouldn't it? You would not have to pay for your fun at all'.

Alice Kelly had no intention of making this easy for Robert O' Connor.

'And, isn't it your responsibility to care for the child and me? After all, you are the father'.

Robert was beginning to feel cornered. It was not a nice feeling at all.

He desperately needed some hope of escape.

'I have only your word for that, and I have only your word that you are pregnant at all. I mean, you haven't even gone to the doctor yet'.

The more he talked, the more belligerent Alice became. It stung her that her honesty was being called into question.

'Come on then, you come with me to the dispensary in the morning, if you don't believe me and you'll soon learn the truth'.

'Alright then, you are pregnant, but who's to say it's not some other man's child?'

Robert could see that he was only aggravating the situation and doing his case no good at all.

'What I mean is, it could be Edward's baby?'

'God bless the innocence of that God-fearing brother of yours. Unless it was wished into my womb, he had nothing to do with it. From what I saw of him in the hospital, it will be a long time before he has sex on his mind. Robert, there is no earthly doubt that I am pregnant with your child. I am insisting that you do the right thing and set things right by me'.

Robert was in no doubt about where she saw her future, but he had no desire to travel down that particular road.

'If you mean getting married, I can tell you that I have no notion of marrying you. We are not well matched, and in no time at all, we would be killing each other'.

That unlikely scenario did nothing to make Alice reconsider her strategy.

'You were not saying that when you got me pregnant. We were matched pretty well then. Anyway, we will be as well matched as most married couples around here'.

Robert was becoming so desperate that he even visualised coming clean with Katie. However, no matter how he tried he could never imagine himself telling her that he had been unfaithful with Alice. One way or another, Robert was determined that he would never walk down the aisle with Alice Kelly, baby or no baby. As he looked at the woman who threatened his future happiness, he only felt anger and hatred. However, his usually reliable instincts dictated that he should say or do nothing for the moment, and hope things might miraculously work out.

He was sure about two things. He was never going to face Katie with the news that he had fathered Alice's child, and secondly, he was never going to marry Alice Kelly.

Chapter 48

Robert considered that Edward had improved in appearance. He had put on a little weight and his face had filled out, giving him a healthier look. Dressed in his Sunday clothes and sitting upright on the chair in the visiting room, he could have passed for a gentleman receiving guests into his stately home.

'I wondered when you might come', Edward said in a calm, matter of fact manner.

Robert was pleasantly surprised that he had been received so civilly and felt the need to apologise for not visiting him sooner.

'I would have come weeks ago but people thought that it might not be good in your condition. It would be like a....'

'A red rag to a bull, you mean'.

Edward finished the sentence for him, with a trace of a smile on his upper lip.

Despite Edward's incarceration, he was well aware of the date.

'It's Halloween night. I suppose they'll be devilment around the place tonight, with gates being taken off and all sorts of tricks being played'.

'You can bet on it', Robert answered.

'There's always lads putting slates on chimney pots to smoke the houses or hiding in the hedges, rattling chains when anyone comes along'.

Edward sat more upright in his seat. There was a flicker of interest or excitement in his eyes.

'Jaysus. I just realise you will be sleeping at the graveyard on Halloween Night. Are you not afraid you'll get a visit?'

Robert was pleased that Edward was so alert and aware of the night in question.

'The dead are harmless. It's the living that we have to worry about'. Edward eased back into his chair again. For a moment or two, he appeared to be considering what his younger brother had said.

'You are right, I suppose. The dead are unlikely to come around with a paint can and leave a message on your gable wall'.

Robert fixed his brother in a stare. He wondered whether this remark had been just an attempt at humour or had he just admitted his guilt? In light of the circumstances, he allowed the remark to pass unchallenged. Before he spoke again, Robert cleared his throat.

'Look here, Edward, I'm sorry if anything I said or did was the cause of you ...em'.

'You mean, cracking up?' Edward asked bluntly.

'Maybe it did or maybe it didn't, I don't know. Anyway, in this place they tell me, it's only the future that matters. The past is gone and there is not a thing we can do to change that. We have to accept it and move on. That's what Dr Smith says anyway'.

Robert was surprised by Edward's positive attitude.

He felt that maybe a question about Alice might sensitively be put to him.

'Alice told me that she was in here last night. Had she any news?' He was interested to know if she had mentioned anything about being pregnant, but considered that to be extremely unlikely.

'Like what? She's not thinking of leaving the country or getting married, is she?

Robert's blood ran cold at the mention of Alice and marriage in the same sentence.

He assured his brother that he had meant local and district news.

'Oh, I see. No, not really. She was on about Mrs Gallagher falling off her bike'.

'Oh yea, that was a bad accident. She broke her wrist, but she'll be right as rain'.

That gave Robert an opening to chance a question about the possibility of getting back with Alice soon. That could help solve Robert's major problem.

'Hopefully you will as right as rain in the near future too. Who knows, maybe Alice and yourself might be back together?'

Edward had been advised well by the professionals and surprisingly, he had no qualms about sharing their advice with his brother.

'They tell me that it would be a mistake to get into any serious relationship for a fair while after I get out. Wounds have to heal, they say, and that doesn't happen overnight'.

Edward had never spoken a truer word. Robert had been given his answer, but not the answer he wanted.

Any lingering hope that Edward could assist him in escaping from his dire predicament was now dead in the water. His brother was in surprisingly good shape, but he was not fully back to his old self and would not be in a position to dash down the aisle with Alice on his left arm.

Now that Robert had the situation clarified, he had little else to say. There followed quite a long lull in the conversation that was broken by Edward.

'I suppose you and Katie are still on for February'.

Edward was better informed than Robert could have imagined. The nature of the question shocked Robert, as did the rather casual way he posed the question. It was a long way from the hostile and belligerent Edward of some weeks ago.

In answering, Robert decided to keep it casual as if they were discussing the date for a variety concert or gymkhana.

'Yea, still on for February,' he answered in as matter of fact tone as he could manage. Edward remained silent for a moment, as he stared into the mid distance over his brother's shoulder. When he spoke it was in more hushed tones as if there were someone likely to be eavesdropping.

'Will you tell Katie that I was asking for her, and that I would love her to visit me soon'.

This was a big ask, and Robert was unsure about how to answer. Edward sensed his apprehension, and felt the need to reassure his brother.

'There will be no trouble from me. Make sure to tell her that, won't you', he added holding Robert in a fixed gaze.

Robert felt that he had to respond to the request.

'I'll tell her what you said. She can make up her own mind on the matter'.

Edward did not push his luck any further. The reply was probably as much as he could have hoped for.

From Robert's position, the business of the meeting had been transacted.

After a meaningless exchange on the subject of the weather, Robert bid farewell to his brother, before heading out into the chilly night. While he was pleased to see that Edward was on the mend, his main focus was on the dilemma facing him.

Robert had some serious thinking to do and the clock was ticking. Time was not his friend.

Chapter 49

After work on Friday, Robert discovered a letter pushed under his door. There wasn't a letterbox on the door, but the gap between the door and floor was more than sufficient to facilitate delivery of a decent sized envelope, not to mention a major-sized draught.

The letter bore an English postmark. He presumed that it was from Billy Parkes even though the handwriting was unfamiliar.

Robert tore open the envelope and moved to the kitchen table to peruse its contents.

As he read, the colour slowly drained from his face as the shocking contents registered.

The signature on the letter was that of a Ronald Baxter, an ex-soldier, close friend and housemate of one Billy Parkes, who departed this life having suffered a fatal fall from the third storey of a construction site in Ealing, West London.

Baxter reported that Billy had clung to life for a number of hours after the fall, but realistically, there was never a genuine prospect of a recovery.

Apparently the man had been going through Billy's stuff, and had seen Robert's letter to Billy. He knew that the two men had been close friends.

'He spoke frequently of you and your shared war experiences. There was no doubting the bond between you.

I am sorry to be the bearer of such sad tidings but I felt that you should know. Chin up, Mate, and raise a glass for Billy tonight.

Yours in sadness,

Ronald Baxter.

Robert sat transfixed, just staring at the page.

The full import of the contents slowly, but surely registered with him. Not only had he lost his closest pal from his army days, but he had also lost his last means of escape if his already dire situation were to become desperate.

The thought of his friend meeting such an early and horrific end sickened his stomach, but the sudden death carried extra significance for him.

Robert O'Connor was alone in fighting whatever Alice Kelly might throw at him, and he was fresh out of both ammunition and an exit strategy.

Thirty minutes later, tears still in his eyes, Robert lifted the latch on the door and walked in the direction of the nearest watering hole. He felt that he should raise a glass or two to Billy's memory. Deep down, he knew that he would continue to drink until he had reached the welcome state of oblivion.

Chapter 50

Robert never made it to the hotel. Some hundred yards or so from his cottage, he encountered Katie on her way there. She could see that he was in an emotional state. With some difficulty, she persuaded him to return to the cottage and try to process the terrible news.

'Getting drunk will give a giant hangover in the morning, and the pain of Billy's death will be as raw as ever when you eventually sober up'.

Back in the cottage, Katie set about brewing a strong pot of tea for him. She always heard that strong tea with added sugar was good for shock.

Robert knew the limitations of such a beverage, but he sipped away at the steaming mug.

Katie had also heard that it was good to talk about one's loss. Bottling it up would be very bad for Robert. Katie was keen to get him to talk about his relationship with Billy Parkes.

Through his tears, Robert answered as best he could. Katie genuinely felt for his loss. Mourning a loved one was something she could easily identify with.

Over the following hours, Robert gradually regained his composure. He felt grateful for Katie's presence, and was pleased that he had not spent the night drinking in the hotel bar. Alcohol dulls the mind and the last thing he needed now was a dull mind. His mind needed to be as sharp as it could possibly be if he were to come up with a solution to his problems.

The sudden death of his army buddy forced him into a reflective mood. He started to question what life was all about. Billy had survived the fury of the war, and yet died a tragically young death in such a peaceful environment. If there were a God above he had a most outrageous sense of irony.

'Where is the letter? Katie asked.

Robert had the letter in his pocket, but was not keen on sharing it. He threw a few decoy glances around the room.

'I left it over there somewhere. It's probably under the papers there', he said pointing to some back editions of the local paper.

He made a few efforts at checking out a few other nooks and crannies but naturally unearthed nothing.

'Maybe you put it in your pocket', Katie suggested.

Robert made an elaborate pretence of rummaging in his pockets but there was no letter for Katie to peruse.

'Ah don't mind. If it never reappears, I'm sure it will be too soon for you', she supposed.

Katie sat holding Robert in her arms and offering him whatever comfort she could. Inevitably, duty would call her.

'I'll soon have to leave you, Robert. Mother will be worried about me out late, and in a little while it will be All Souls' Day. Walking in the dark alongside a graveyard on All Souls' Day would put the heart crossways in me'.

Robert got to his feet.

'Come on. I will walk you home or cycle with you if you prefer'.

'No way! You need to go to bed and have a good rest'.

Robert was determined. He convinced her that there was no way that he would let her travel alone that night. It was a straight choice between staying with him in the cottage or his escorting her home. Predictably, Katie chose the latter.

'If only this were February. I could stay over and be there for you', she sighed.

'Well, it is November, so are you coming or going?'

'I am going. My mother would be demented with worry, and I would not put her through any more pain. But, I hope I was good company for you tonight. It's good to have someone to talk things through with'.

Robert swallowed hard and smiled an acknowledgement.

Katie presumed that his tears were for his deceased friend, but his tears were for himself.

He was on a pathway to unrelenting misery unless he took some evasive action.

Having Alice dictate his future was not something he would tolerate. He must ensure that he become master of his own destiny again.

Chapter 51

The predicted hard frost arrived with a vengeance. From midweek the rain reappeared, but night temperatures remained unseasonably low. Road and street surfaces remained treacherous, with the weak November sun struggling to achieve any semblance of a thaw.

On Friday morning conditions were at their very worst. Heavy drizzle fell during the early hours of the morning, but the skies cleared and freezing temperatures again took hold. By seven o'clock, the main street of the village had taken on a sheen that testified to its treacherous nature.

Most villagers remained indoors waiting for the thaw to take hold. However, some hardy worshippers inched their way up the gentle incline to the church to attend morning Mass. Delighted children used the hill at the top of the street as a runway to propel their descent on a wonderful slide, that took them down past the Garda barracks and on down towards the village hall.

Robert thought it better to leave his bicycle at home, and instead walked to work. However, he had more on his mind than icy pavements. Alice had him demented by her constant pressuring him to do the decent thing by her. It was Robert's instinct to play for time, but time was in short supply for Alice. The moment of reckoning could not be postponed indefinitely. He had to face up to his responsibilities or do the cowardly thing and do a runner.

If only, there were another option.

Robert felt like a cornered rat, and could see no way out of his dire predicament. He felt he had to attack before Alice Kelly ruined him and his future with Katie Higgins. He had to act quickly before the world discovered the truth about him.

In his demented state, he had convinced himself that Alice Kelly was the enemy. She had shown herself to be vindictive and selfish. She had been given a chance to bring this business to an end and she had not taken it. The girl seemed determined to shame him and ruin any prospect of future happiness. He had come to the conclusion that she had over-played her hand and needed to be stopped.

Robert felt that he had to break the stranglehold she had over him. While she carried that baby, she possessed a hold over him.

The bottom line, as he saw it, was that Alice was blackmailing him, and was using her pregnancy to do so.

He surmised that, if she were to accidentally lose that baby, then she would be forever silenced. A single girl in a conservative rural village in 1946 was unlikely to call attention to her pregnancy.

Robert had worked himself into a state of frenzy. He considered that his very survival was at stake. It had come down to a choice between fight or flight. He made a decision to stay and fight.

It was imperative to find some way of neutralising Alice's threat. In acting against her, it was important to do so without causing additional problems for him.

With drastic situations calling for drastic remedies, the madcap idea presented itself. It was as if the universe had come to his assistance in the form of the treacherous conditions underfoot. These conditions could be used to his advantage.

The decision was made. All that was necessary was for him to be in the right place at the right time.

He knew that each morning around eleven o'clock, Alice crossed over to the butcher's stall to collect the meat order. Robert's plan involved waiting until Alice started her return trip. He would then make his move. While appearing to assist the girl across the road, he would pretend to slip on the slippery surface, and drag her to the ground as forcefully as he could. If his plan were successful, her leverage over him would be gone forever. Not once, in his agitated state, did he identify with the baby she was carrying.

Some moments after eleven o'clock, Robert observed Alice inch her way across the frozen street, before entering the butcher's shop. There would follow a few moments delay before her return trip. Business was slow at the meat counter, so the butcher had ample time to engage Alice in conversation. As he watched them, Robert could imagine that the weather was the number one topic of conversation. He wished she would hurry up and return with her purchases before some brave customer arrived looking to buy some material from the yard.

Anxiety gripped him as he waited for her to start her return trip. After about ten minutes, the door of the butcher's shop swung open again. Alice left with her parcel of meat, and began the hazardous return trip. This was Robert's cue to act.

He must not give the game away.

He needed to sound natural and convincing to Alice and anyone else who might overhear him.

'Come on, Alice, give me the parcel, and grab a hold of me. These streets are deadly'.

Alice was pleasantly surprised by the cheery banter and the gentlemanly gesture. She handed the parcel of meat over to Robert and linked her arm into his.

'Why thank you, Mr O'Connor. You know, I could get used to this attention'.

Robert checked all around him before he started to walk. He hoped that there would be someone to witness the accident that was about to unfold.

He could not believe his luck when the best witness possible suddenly appeared on the scene. Garda Casey was just a few yards away carefully picking his steps on the frozen footpath. Robert turned towards him and timed his greeting to perfection.

There would now be a witness to the upcoming accident.

A few seconds later, Robert simulated a slip that took his feet from under him. His right foot deliberately caught Alice's left leg and successfully upended her.

Unfortunately for Robert, his slip badly backfired on him. What had initially been a contrived movement soon became a genuine accident, as the impetus of the fall swept him right off his feet and tossed him, like a ragdoll, onto the footpath. His left leg smashed onto the ground and his head smashed off the kerb. Then, he became conscious of a heavy weight falling on top of him.

When Robert finally regained consciousness, he was lying on the ground with a small but growing number of people around him. The accident had brought many of the locals out of doors. He scanned the faces of those around him, and to Robert's horror, he saw that Alice Kelly was one of those people.

More alarmingly for Robert, she seemed to have emerged unscathed from her fall.

Suddenly, he became conscious of a rather painful wound to his right temple. He could feel blood running down from the wound and onto his neck. His injured leg was very painful also, but the greatest pain came with the realisation that his dastardly plan had completely failed.

It was now only a matter of time before he would be exposed as the unfaithful fiancé. Only that his leg was injured, he would have got to his feet and made a run for it.

Dr Clarke had been summoned and he began to examine him as best he could under the circumstances.

'Robert, I heard you took a little tumble and injured yourself. Alice tells me that you were doing the gentlemanly thing in assisting her. I am pretty sure that your leg is fractured, so Guard Casey is organising an ambulance to take you to the hospital. When you are admitted, I will get them to take a look at your head too, because we can't be too careful where the head is concerned'.

Robert found himself drifting in and out of consciousness. An ambulance crew used a splint for his injured leg, before lifting him onto a stretcher. He heard Mr Murphy's voice, wishing him a speedy recovery. Already, Robert knew that he would never work for the man again or for anyone else in the area. Alice would still insist that he marry her and that was one thing he would never do. If Katie were to find out about Alice and him, their engagement would be off. He would have to leave the area and leave quickly, but a man can't run very far with a broken leg.

The condition of the roads meant that the journey to Sligo County Hospital took longer than usual. As soon as he was admitted, arrangements were put into place for surgery on his leg, but it was his head injury that most concerned the attending medic. His blood pressure reading gave serious cause for concern and so arrangements for orthopaedic surgery were put on hold. Robert's vital signs were giving some cause for concern. The medics conferred as to the best way to proceed. This was proving to be no straightforward case.

Chapter 52

A highly stressed Katie Higgins arrived at the hospital at approximately three o'clock. Robert's employer, Joseph accompanied her. The girl at the desk directed Katie to an observation ward, down a long corridor to the right. As she hurried along, the smell of cleansing fluids in her nostrils evoked bitter memories of her late father's time in Manorhamilton hospital.

Mr Murphy sought to be optimistic.

'Don't you worry, Robert will be as right as rain long before February'.

When they arrived at the door of his ward, the nurse insisted that no visitors were allowed. However, on discovering that she was the patient's fiancée, the nurse reluctantly allowed Katie to sit with him for a few moments.

'Robert is in a serious condition, and he is not to be disturbed'.

Alarm bells began to ring for Katie, as she held Robert's hand in hers. This had all come as a terrible shock for her. She had been led to believe that his condition called for no more than routine surgery. Now, the medics were really concerned for his welfare.

A few moments, later Mr Murphy, following a signal from the nurse, persuaded Katie to leave the room.

'Come on Katie, we are only in the way here. How about we take a cup of tea and come back a bit later when they might have an update for you'.

Katie released Robert's hand from her grasp and followed Mr Murphy to his car.

He drove her into town and brought her to the *Cafe Cairo* to while away the time until the hospital had more information on Robert's condition.

Murphy tried to make pleasant conversation.

'I like this place and generally call in here whenever I'm in Sligo'.

Katie sat down at a table oblivious to what establishment she was in. She stared morosely into the mid-distance and reflected on the tragic turn of events. Mr Murphy ordered a pot of strong tea and some sandwiches in the vain hope that she might eat something.

Food was the last thing on Katie's mind. She found it difficult to accept that only yesterday, she had excitedly discussed wedding plans with Robert. He had seemed a little distracted, but still appeared to be in good spirits. Less than twenty-four hours later, he was lying in hospital with possible life-threatening injuries. That was difficult for her to get her head around.

She cursed the ice and the weather that had caused the accident. She had learned from Mr Murphy that Robert had been escorting Alice across the frosty street when he had lost his footing in the slippery conditions. Alice had emerged unscathed, and ironically, Robert's body cushioned her fall.

'That's just typical. Isn't it? No act of kindness goes unpunished'.

Mr Murphy did his best to jolly her along with some optimistic scenarios, but his efforts proved fruitless. She was growing more impatient by the moment, and was eager to return to the hospital as quickly as possible. Under pressure from Murphy, she reluctantly agreed to gulp down a few mouthfuls of strong tea to help steady her nerves, but she had no appetite for sandwiches. Neither did she countenance Murphy's suggestion that they pop into one of the neighbouring premises for a small brandy, purely for medicinal purposes, of course.

"I know you mean well, Mr Murphy but unless you drive me back up to the hospital now, I will walk there myself.'

Faced with such determination and insistence, there was nothing for it except to drive up The Mall to Sligo County Hospital.

On arrival, it was soon clear that Robert's condition had deteriorated considerably.

The nurse hurried to meet her.

'Thank God, you came back. We were desperately trying to locate you'.

Katie now feared the worst. The serious-faced nurse led them into a side room and invited them to sit down, before telling Katie that a senior doctor would speak to her in a moment.

When he arrived, the doctor's expression was sombre.

'I am very sorry to tell you that Robert did not make it. We tried our best to save him, but his internal injuries were so serious that they proved fatal'.

Katie collapsed in a bundle with the devastating news. The doctor's words had shattered her world. After so much promise, her future now held nothing but emptiness and loss for her. The love of her life had been cruelly taken from her. She had been robbed of her chance to walk down the aisle with him and become Katie O' Connor. Her life, up to then, had been relatively problem free. Now, in a short space of time, the two men she loved most had been taken from her. She never imagined that life could be so cruel. What had she done to deserve all this pain?

She was angry with Robert for leaving her again. She wished that she could die too and be buried with him. At least, they would be united in death.

Chapter 53

Robert was laid out in his parents' house. Tommy and Julia gave up their downstairs bedroom to facilitate the viewing of their son's remains. Their bed had been stripped of its usual bedding, and replaced by the best of Irish linen, which Julia had kept in her bottom drawer for such occasions. A hand-quilted bedspread lay across the bed. Robert lay, as he laid in life, youthful and handsome, with rosary beads entwined around his fingers. The gaudy scar on his temple seemed to have faded, thanks to the efforts of Julia and Norah with a little help from Mrs Carrington's make up bag.

For the duration of her son's involvement in the war she had entertained the terrible dread that such a tragedy might befall him. The irony of the situation was not lost on her. Her son had survived the bullets and the shells of the war, only to come a cropper on the deserted main street of their peaceful village.

Neighbours and friends filed into the room, offering silent prayers for the happy repose of the young man's soul before shaking hands with family members. All professed to be very sorry for their trouble. The parish priest prayed over the remains and offered whatever spiritual consolation he could. Dr Clarke also called and extended his sympathy to the family. He offered medication that might help dull the sharp pain of loss. This offer was politely declined.

The one constant in that front room, apart from the corpse, was the person of Katie Higgins. She rarely lifted her eyes from the remains of her fiancé. At times she touched his hands. At other times she cried sad, bitter tears, but mostly she sat transfixed. Over and over in her mind she had asked herself why this had happened?

She wondered why God had frustrated her just when happiness was almost within her grasp. Her wedding date was only a few short months away. What sort of day would February 14, St Valentine's Day be for her now?

Every year for the rest of her life that day would be a dark one, even if she were to live to a ripe old age. Right now, she had no future to consider. There was only the pain and sorrow, with no prospect of there being anything different to come.

Julia and Tommy were beyond consoling. Tommy spent most of his time, with head bowed in anguish, looking up occasionally to silently acknowledge the sympathy of callers. Julia cried and cried until all that were left to her were tearless sighs and lamentations. A matter of weeks ago, she had two healthy sons.

Now one lay dead and the other was still incarcerated in a mental asylum. Edward would be present for the removal and burial, but it was a heavy cross for her to bear. Her daughter Norah had temporarily moved back into the house to support her parents over the wake and funeral. Her new husband, Hughie helped dig Robert's grave in the O'Connor plot.

His final resting place was just a matter of yards from the cottage he had rented. Alice could not find it in herself to view Robert's remains. She blamed herself for the accident. It had been such an innocuous incident, and yet a man lay dead because of it. Alice had other concerns too. Her entire future was shrouded in doubt. At one time, it almost seemed possible that she could have her choice of Edward or Robert as a husband.

Now she could have neither. She could have no other man either if it became known that she was pregnant.

Immediately, after the fall on the ice she had visited Dr Clarke to put her mind at ease concerning the baby. Part of her wished that the baby might be no more. It would have saved much heartache in the long term. However, the baby was alive and developing well. Alice was the mother of Robert O' Connor's baby, but she was in no position to raise that child on her own.

She had her mind made up that she would leave the area immediately after the funeral. She would spin some semi-plausible story to her family. That would be preferable to the inevitable finger wagging and the unwanted pity.

Chapter 54

On November 11 after eleven o'clock Mass in St. Patrick's Church, the remains of Robert O'Connor were brought the short distance to his last resting place in Creevelea Abbey to be buried alongside his paternal grandparents. The fact that it was the eleventh hour of the eleventh day of the eleventh month was not lost on the congregation. In a strange way it too marked an end to hostilities for Robert O' Connor.

As his coffin was lowered into the earth, the parish priest reminded all of those assembled there that, like the deceased, they too would return to the dust.

In his homily, Fr Maguire had spoken of the deceased, as a young man with an independent streak, who was not unduly worried about what other people might think of him. He summed him up in six short words.

'Robert danced to his own tune'.

There were few to argue with his summation.

Robert's parents cut a forlorn sight as they huddled together for comfort in the bitterly cold November air. Edward stood alongside them. He had been granted day-release for the funeral. It was clear from his appearance that his road to recovery would be somewhat longer than had been previously envisaged.

Katie Higgins stood some yards away flanked by her mother and brother. A few short months earlier, she had buried her father, but that enormous grief paled into insignificance, with what she was experiencing as she looked into the open grave of her one true love

The harsh scraping sound of the shovels on the stony clay sent a shiver down her spine. Worse still however was the thud of the clay on the lid of the coffin as the grave was filled. While most of the mourners opted to take the shortcut back to the village, Katie chose to walk one last time to the humble cottage she had hoped to share with Robert when she became Katie O' Connor.

As she rounded the corner, she could see that someone else had the same idea.

Alice, now that she had been observed, waited for Katie to catch up with her. After a rather awkward moment, with neither knowing what to say, the two women embraced warmly. It seems that neither of them was destined to be Mrs O'Connor.

The two heartbroken women parted and went their separate ways. Their futures seemed to offer little but the pain of loneliness and regret, but as they were still alive, they had to grit their teeth and get on with it.

.